OVER THE EDGE

SUSAN K. DRONEY

This is a work of fiction. Names, characters, places, and incidents are products of the author's imagination or are used fictitiously and are not to be construed as real. Any resemblance to actual events, locations, organizations, or persons, living or dead, is entirely coincidental.

World Castle Publishing, LLC
Pensacola, Florida
Copyright © Susan K. Droney 2016
Paperback ISBN: 9781629894805
eBook ISBN: 9781629894812
First Edition World Castle Publishing, LLC, June 27, 2016
http://www.worldcastlepublishing.com
Licensing Notes
Cover: Karen Fuller
Editor: Maxine Bringenberg

PROLOGUE

She watched from her vantage point, crouched by the side of his car, her eyes fixed on his front door. The gun felt good in her grip. Swallowing hard, she removed the safety.

The door slowly opened, and a dark figure emerging through the shadows made her heart quicken. He lit a cigarette, throwing the match on the ground as he walked toward his car. She sucked in her breath as her finger tightened on the trigger, then quickly pulled it.

He slumped to the ground. Slowly she walked to the body and stood over him. He looked up at her and tried to speak, but all she heard were moans gurgling up from his throat. She looked into his terrorized eyes, satisfied that the last thing he saw was no compassion in her own, and then with a boot-clad foot, kicked him in the ribs, being careful to avoid the blood seeping through his shirt. "Bet you thought you'd never see me again," she sneered as she aimed the gun at his forehead then pulled the trigger again.

CHAPTER ONE

Maggie Allen stood behind the counter eyeing the customers beginning to fill the booths. She grabbed her order pad and a pencil. A familiar couple seated themselves in her station. Inwardly, she seethed with anger as she watched them, but outwardly, she was bright and cheerful. She hated having to put on a false front but knew it was a requisite of the job to treat all of her customers with friendliness, even those she couldn't stomach.

"Hi, Brant. Janna," she said in the cheeriest voice she could muster. She flipped the order pad to a clean page. "What can I get you two?"

"Coffee. Hon?" The man nodded toward the beautiful petite blond at his side.

"The same." She smiled at Maggie. "Did you hear about our new house?"

Maggie looked into her sparkling baby blue eyes. "Yes, I hear it's quite a showplace." She forced a tight smile. She'd

7

give anything to be called away from their table instead of enduring their phony attempts at friendliness. They were up to something. That she was sure of.

"You and Chris should come over some night for dinner and we'll give you the grand tour," Janna gushed, dramatically throwing her arms up in a flamboyant gesture. "It's like a palace!" She gripped Brant's arm. "We never dreamed it would be so beautiful! Did we, honey?"

Brant smiled keeping his eyes glued on Maggie, but Maggie knew he was hoping for some reaction from her.

"Promise me you'll visit very soon," Janna continued.

"Thanks, Janna," Maggie said with the same tight smile. Now she was certain that the invitation was given only for Brant's satisfaction. There had to be an ulterior motive behind it. Any gesture of kindness from those two usually came with a high price. She looked at Brant, but his finely chiseled face gave her no clue as his steely gray eyes peered back at her with a rigid and pretentious smile on his lips. He reminded her of a drill sergeant.

Her father had looked like that—always barking out orders and waiting for everyone to kowtow to his inhuman demands. He lived by only one set of rules—his own—and damned be the person who dared disobey him. Her life growing up with him had been hell, and she'd always felt she was raised in a prison camp instead of a seemingly normal to the outside world middle-class home with all the comforts and luxuries to satisfy any child. If her father hadn't been in the picture, she would have had an almost perfect childhood under her mother's care.

She hadn't been happy and consequently hadn't felt loved. She'd tried to get close to her father so many times, but the frigid atmosphere around him kept her at bay, thus keeping her from getting to know him and him from getting to know her. As far as she was concerned, he was only the man whose sperm had given her life. There was no love or bonding between them, and he seemed contented to keep their relationship that way, so she accepted it.

Her mother defended him until the day she died, telling Maggie that she should try to get to know him. It had never done Maggie any good trying to talk to her mother about him. In her mother's eyes, her father was perfect and always would be. She loved him, and it was a love Maggie couldn't understand. Occasionally, though, she would catch her mother with a far-off look in her eye. At those times, her eyes were filled with such sadness that Maggie wondered what really was in her mother's heart. After her mother's death, the relationship with her father deteriorated even further. He was a stranger, and their relationship was not destined to change.

She mourned her mother's passing and suffered alone while her father buried himself in his work, and she buried herself in her studies. She missed the long talks and the comforting shoulder her mother freely offered when the high school frustrations of life became too much for her. She filled the void with her friends and activities as her father distanced himself further from her. He provided the necessities of life to her, but little more.

When her father died, she never shed a tear at his funeral, but instead felt relieved watching his casket slowly entering the freshly dug grave. She hated him for all the pain he'd brought to her life, but mostly for never apologizing for that pain. When he died suddenly from a heart attack, she was left alone in the world with no one to give her advice, good or bad. She set out to make her mark in the world and had until life dealt her a terrible blow. Now she was here, but Brant would never let her forget where she'd been.

"I'll get your coffee," she said, breaking Brant's penetrating gaze. She returned a couple of minutes later with their beverages. She set the cups on the table and then made a hasty departure.

As she waited on customers, she occasionally stole glances at Janna and Brant. They had no intention of following up on the invitation. It was just another slap in the face to let her know that they had money, success, and power. Their new house was one more bitter reminder to her of all she had lost. They infuriated her, and their only purpose for ever stopping in the diner was to rub her nose in it. She looked disgustedly at them in their designer clothes amid the regulars who were usually clad in jeans and T-shirts.

Cedar Pines, Pennsylvania was the type of city, which distinctly separated its citizens into two groups—those who had wealth and those who did not. If you fell in the middle somewhere, as did most of the inhabitants, then you lived on the other side of town with the have-nots. But if there was a chance you could move up the social ladder, you might be able to live on the edge of the wealthy.

Brant was a dark, handsome, well-conditioned, thirty-year-old detective in the Cedar Pines Police Department. His salary could never afford him the luxuries he craved, but Janna, at the tender age of twenty-five, was another story. Her inherited wealth matched her beauty—she had too much of both and was not afraid to use either if it got her what she wanted. Brant didn't care whom he used or hurt to satisfy his own selfish desires. When Janna and Brant married, it was a union destined to destroy many lives. They were a formidable team, and God help anyone who got in their way.

She stared hard at the both of them sitting on their thrones using their looks and money to draw attention to themselves. She saw the empty shallowness they both possessed on the inside and knew that someday when their outside beauty faded, if they didn't change their ways, there would be no inner beauty to shine through. They would be two selfish, miserable human beings. Her prophecies brought her little comfort now, though, as she struggled through each day of her life.

"Remember to give us a call when you have a free evening, Maggie," Janna said brightly as Brant squeezed a few bills into her hand. "Keep the change." He tipped his hat.

Maggie struggled to maintain her composure. "I'll let Chris know." She watched their departure.

Shelly Burgess squeezed her arm. "They're quite a pair."

"Yes, but a pair of what?" Maggie replied with a cunning grin as she looked at her co-worker's pretty face. She liked Shelly. She was a slightly overweight but very hardworking single mother of two active boys, Tommy and Terry. Her main goal in life was to raise her boys with the best she could possibly give them. Her wonderful sense of humor and wholesome friendliness immediately drew people to her.

Shelly laughed and the dimples in her cheeks became prominent. "I hate people like them, especially Janna. She doesn't have a clue what it's like to have to pinch pennies just to keep a roof over your head and food on the table." She sighed wistfully. "I've always wondered why some people have everything and others have to work and struggle so damned hard for everything." Her eyes narrowed. "It seems so unfair. Every time I try to put something into the boys'

11

college fund, I get hit with an unexpected expense. It seems like I can never win."

"I know how you feel, Shell." Her eyes sparkled. "However, your two little boys are the best gifts you could ever ask for, and nothing in this world or any amount of money could even compare to the joy you get from them."

She smiled. "I know, and I thank God every single day for them. I just wish I could do more for them. I don't want them to have just the basic necessities of life." She sighed. "I know I'm such a cliché, but I do want to give them the moon!"

"You already have. The love you give them is worth more than any material things. The quality time you spend playing and talking with them means more than any toy ever could. They may not see it now, but someday they will, and these times are what they'll always remember—the happy times they spent with their mom."

"Whenever I'm feeling doubtful, you always put things into the proper perspective for me, Maggie."

"That's what I'm here for, my dear," she said with a wide grin.

Shelly laughed. "You're definitely one of a kind."

She patted Shelly's arm as a pensive look came over her face. "I wonder if Janna was close to her parents growing up. She mentioned nannies and servants as being an integral part of her life, but come to think of it, she never talked about doing things with her parents as a family. That's so sad if the people you were closest to were nannies and servants instead of your own mother and father."

"It must have been lonely for her, even though she'd probably never admit it to anyone."

"I'm sure it was, and you're right. She'd never let on if it had bothered her. My father is another story, but I remember my mother always being there for me. Some of my fondest memories are when I'd spend hours in the kitchen baking with her and she'd listen to all of my troubles. We'd sit late at night in front of a crackling fire, and she patiently taught me how to sew. That's what I mean about what you're doing now with Terry and Tommy, honey."

Shelly nodded. "I guess I'm lucky because I've always been close to both of my parents. Maybe that's part of my problem. I'm trying too hard to be the boys' mother and father." She ran a hand through her short-cropped brown hair. "I know my parents want to help the boys and me, and as much as I appreciate their offer of help, I want to make it on my own. I need to know that I can do this one thing and do it right. Does that make sense to you, Maggie?" She shrugged. "My parents barely have enough to keep their own heads above water, but they would sacrifice their own needs for me and the boys."

"It makes perfect sense to me. You've got a strong, admirable character, Shelly, and that is a special gift your parents gave you. Not many young women in your situation would feel the way you do, but instead would probably try to grab everything they could get their hands on. Your extraordinary strength and values are what you're instilling in your own children. Be proud of that. You're doing a great job with them, the same way your parents did with you."

"Thanks, Maggie." She sighed as she looked at her tables. "Luke needs a refill. Guess I'd better get back to work."

She nodded. "It's going to be a scorcher out there later on so I guess I'd better get some more iced tea going."

****

Later Maggie sat at her kitchen table, a half-eaten salad

in front of her. It was too muggy to eat anything hot. Her window fan and the fan in the corner of the kitchen didn't seem to offer much relief from the stifling heat. It seemed to hang in her small trailer making her feel as though she were trapped inside a metal trunk.

She gazed out of the kitchen window at the thickening clouds then slowly stood up, scraping the chair across the worn linoleum floor. She hoped the impending rainstorm would give some relief to the heat. She was restless tonight, and a feeling of loneliness overtook her. She hated these melancholy moods. Sometimes they'd creep up out of nowhere, almost suffocating her.

She eyed her meager possessions. This was all she had to show for years of her hard work. It hadn't always been this way. Once she had everything she ever wanted or could possibly want, but that seemed like a lifetime ago. Right when she was at the top, an error in judgment caused her to topple and land in a crumpled heap back down at the bottom. All she could do was lie there wondering what had happened and try to claw her way back to the top. But that was never to be again. Her life would have to begin anew.

Today she lived in a tiny, rented, rundown trailer, barely able to afford the monthly rent and utilities. She was grateful to have her job as a waitress, even though it paid only minimum wage plus whatever tips her customers gave her. She had quickly learned that a customer would be more willing to part with his hard-earned cash if she were friendly. In time she felt a distinctive bond growing with the regulars, as they became the family she yearned for, filling the empty void within her. Her friendliness toward them soon became less forced and instead genuinely sincere. She'd grown accustomed to their stories and jokes, and when they talked about their families and adventures, she felt like she was a part of their lives.

The brightest spot in her life was Chris Jacoby. He filled the longing in her that no man had ever been able to. He was the strength she lacked and the passion she desired. She looked out the window again as the first drops of rain began to fall and wondered where Chris was tonight. He worked too hard on and off the job, trying his best to give the material comforts she lacked, but most importantly, the love she so desperately craved. Lately he'd become distant, and it worried her. Maybe she was so naïve and desperate to hold onto him that she couldn't pick up the signals anymore. Her insecurities gnawed at her.

For the past couple of months Chris had barely touched her, and she'd convinced herself that he was just tired from the long hours with his construction job. After all, the nice weather provided the go-ahead on many projects that had been held up because of the prolonged winter weather. Doubt slowly crept in. Could the real reason for his aloofness be that he just wasn't interested in her anymore and didn't know how to tell her?

Had she missed every sign he'd been putting up? Why hadn't she been alert to his late hours and frequent nights out with the guys? It was occurring with increasing frequency. Was that the reason he wouldn't relinquish his apartment and permanently move in with her? Had he grown tired of her? Didn't she matter even a little to him? Could he just walk away and forget what they'd shared? Her head throbbed, and she rubbed her aching temples wishing she could shut out her screaming fears.

Chapter Two

Chelsea Howard lay seductively on the bed watching Chris empty out his pockets. He carefully placed the items on the bureau. She patted the spot next to her. "Coming to bed, honey?"

He kept his back to her. "I'm going to grab a shower." His voice was without feeling.

"I'll be waiting. Don't be long," she purred running her hands down her long slender legs.

He shot her a disgusted look as he made his way into the bathroom. When he closed the door, he saw his reflection staring back at him in the full-length mirror on the back of the door. He studied his face realizing that the man staring back at him was a skeleton of his former self. His eyes looked hollow and sunken in, and his normally ruddy, healthy-looking complexion now looked ashen as though he were ill. Then he realized his outside appearance proved the agonizing turmoil inside of him. A battle was being fought within his own heart.

His eyes caught sight of the small counter above the

sink where Chelsea had placed his shaving supplies and deodorant. His toothbrush was in a holder next to hers. He became uncomfortable as he looked around the room. This was not what he wanted or had planned. He rubbed his weary eyes and studied his face again.

Up until a few weeks ago, he was good-looking for his forty-five years, with a healthy head of curly brown hair and a strong muscular build. Aside from the rigorous demands of his job, he kept in shape by going to the gym three times a week and jogging whenever he could. Most people took him to be ten years younger because of his boyish looks and friendly smile.

He recalled how surprised Maggie had been when she'd learned his age. He was a regular patron of Tom's Diner long before Maggie had even begun working there, but from the first moment he'd laid eyes on her, he wanted to know her better. For months he had silently kept a watch on her. He knew she was single because she didn't wear a ring and hadn't mentioned any one particular man in her life, and he hadn't seen any one man paying special attention to her. Later Tom and Shelly confirmed that fact for him.

Maggie was beautiful with auburn hair, sparkling sea-green eyes, and a slim but shapely figure. She always had a friendly smile for him and laughed good-naturedly at his silly jokes. He'd built up a rapport with her over time and then one day realized he was beginning to feel the stirrings of something deeper.

He hadn't had feelings like these in a long time. The last time he'd felt like this over a woman, he'd been crushed when a few days before his wedding day his bride-to-be had been killed in a freak accident. He vowed then to never let another woman come near his heart. He couldn't bear the crushing pain of losing someone again. He'd almost come close to the life he'd always wanted, but when Jill had been so senselessly snatched from him, it forever ended his own dreams, and he felt like he had died along with her in the gas explosion that ripped apart the office building she'd been working in.

He submerged himself in his work, building a reputation as one of the best construction foremen Cedar Pines had ever seen. He'd come from a long line of hard-working men and felt bonded to the city and land where his ancestors had begun. He was an old-fashioned man with old-fashioned ideas. He dated occasionally, but whenever he saw a woman was becoming too emotionally attached and expecting more than he was able to offer, he backed away. He didn't mind being single, but he still sometimes wondered what it would be like to be married with a couple of kids and a wife to come home to every day. His job paid well, but if winters stayed as harsh as the past few had been, the salary sharply declined. He'd learned to budget for the off months and still live comfortably. He'd thought of buying a house, mostly as a project to work on in the winters, but it was just a pipe dream that had disappeared as quickly as Jill had. He didn't put much effort into making it a reality and stayed put in his small bachelor apartment.

He was for the most part contented with the way his life had mapped out in the years since Jill's death. That was until the day he saw Maggie Allen. There was something about her that made his heartbeat quicken. Many times he stopped in the diner just to watch her as she waited on customers. He longed to get to know her better, but outside of the diner. He was surprised that after fifteen years a woman as sweet and fresh as the early morning dew had stolen his heart. He didn't know how it had happened, but then maybe his heart was waiting for the woman who would mend him and make him whole again. He came alive when he talked to Maggie, and all of his dormant emotions exploded to the surface.

It took him weeks to build up the courage to ask her out. He eagerly waited, like a teenage boy with sweating palms, for her answer and was elated when she accepted his invitation. He soon found they had much in common, and at first the twelve-year age difference bothered him, but she constantly assured him that it didn't bother her. He fell completely in love with her before he knew what was happening.

His thoughts took him back to the first time they made love. She was the most passionate, giving woman he had ever known. She possessed a gentleness that made him, watching her from a distance, want to embrace her, thankful that she was his. Just being close to her made his heart skip a beat, and he'd never lost that sensation with the passing of time, instead feeling it only intensify with each new day. There was no denying that this was the woman he wanted to spend his life with, and he'd almost been ready to pop the question when a curveball named Chelsea Howard was thrown at him hurling his whole life out of balance.

He'd never intended to get involved with Chelsea. He wasn't even attracted to her, but one night after he'd finished putting up some bookshelves for her, she'd handed him a cold beer and asked his advice on a personal matter. She was just a kid to him, and he'd only wanted to offer her guidance as a father would to his daughter.

As they talked, she kept supplying the beer and he kept drinking it. She seductively crossed her long slender legs several times as they conversed, and his eyes couldn't help but travel up to her hemline, which showed her young tender thighs. Now looking back, he realized that he was being set up. She'd charmed him and made him feel twenty again, complimenting him on all the areas his male ego loved, inflating him until he was ready for the kill. She'd made him briefly forget that Maggie was the only woman he wanted and loved.

He was sick to his very core afterward. There was no excuse for what he'd done, and there was no changing that fact. After their one-night stand, he tried avoiding Chelsea, but she began showing up in the places she knew he'd be. She was a close friend of Janna Evans, and even though Chris had nothing personal against Janna, he couldn't stand her husband Brant. He'd known Brant ever since Brant was a young boy and Chris had been hired to do some remodeling on the Evans' home. During his breaks, Brant would sit asking all kinds of questions. As Chris worked that summer, he thought it odd that Brant had few playmates, but in time, even at such a young age, Brant's nastiness showed through in the way he treated the few boys who came around. He was a selfish, self-centered boy, and as Chris's work on the Evans' home came to an end, Chris realized why the boy was avoided like the plague.

Since that time, Brant had considered Chris a friend and occasionally invited him to social functions. Chris only attended knowing it was better to have Brant for a friend rather than an enemy. Brant's reputation was well known, and his malevolence came full circle when he joined the police department. It didn't take him long to infiltrate his self-absorbed power with a few of his coworkers who secretly shared his wickedness but had been uncertain how to put it to use. That was until Brant Evans came along.

Chris recalled the conversation he'd recently had

with Brant when Brant had unexpectedly shown up at his apartment.

"We need to talk, Jacoby."

Chris eyed him suspiciously knowing from the way he held himself erect and the squaring of his jaw that Brant wasn't in the mood for games. But then, Brant Evans didn't possess even the remotest sense of humor as far as Chris was concerned. "What can I do for you, Brant?"

"You know that my wife and Chelsea are best friends."

He nodded. "I'm aware of that."

Brant leaned against the doorjamb. "It seems we have a problem." He thoughtfully pulled on his chin.

Chris shrugged his shoulders and frowned. "I don't know what you're talking about. Is there something I can help you with?"

Brant laughed. "Get off it, Chris. For God's sake, you don't just fuck a young beauty like Chelsea Howard and walk away. What the hell's the matter with you?"

Chris ran his hand through his hair as the color drained from his face. "What happened between Chelsea and me was a big mistake. For Christ's sake, Brant, she's just a kid. It never should have happened." He emphatically shook his head back and forth wondering why she'd even mentioned that night. He supposed it was another sign of the times that he hated so much. Years ago a woman never would have mentioned the most intimate details of her sexual experiences to her friends. Or at least he'd always assumed that women were above the locker-room mentality of men. "I'll always regret it."

"But it did happen." He squared his shoulders. "She cares about you, Chris. You know how emotional women can get. They're not like us when it comes to sex. Right away they expect us to feel as bonded to them as they become to us." He snickered. "If you don't, then they become all emotional on you. It's like PMS, only it never stops. Send her some flowers or candy to show her you care."

"I don't think about Chelsea that way, Brant. Like I said, it should have never happened."

Brant slowly shook his head. "Now, Chris, what kind of a man are you? You're going to choose an over-the-hill conniving bitch like Maggie Allen instead of a tender young thing like Chelsea?" He scoffed. "What the hell's the matter with you? You've got an opportunity most men would beg for. What does Maggie have that would make you throw away a chance with Chelsea?"

Chris's muscles tensed. "Maggie has something that women like Chelsea will never have, and that's called *class*. You have no right to call Maggie names. Just keep her out of it. You know nothing about her," he angrily replied as his hands formed into tight hard fists.

Brant threw his head back and laughed. "Well, I call it as I see it, and with Maggie I don't see any class, only a washed-up whore who destroyed her life because of her corrupt ways." He sniffed. "Her partner in crime even dumped her when the heat was on."

Chris looked into Brant's devious eyes. "Maggie's past is none of your damned business. She was set up! The bastard used her!"

Brant continued to laugh. "Boy, she certainly has you hoodwinked." His eyes narrowed. "You've been pussy-whipped for too long."

Chris shook with rage. He lost control over one of his clenched fists, which suddenly came up and with a resounding thud when flesh meets flesh, connected powerfully with

Brant's jaw.

Brant stumbled backward. "You're going to be sorry for that, buddy," he warned rubbing his jaw as he walked to his car. "You can count on it!"

Chris knew that Brant's ax would eventually fall on him. He just didn't know when or how, only that it would. Brant would never allow anyone in Cedar Pines to gain the upper hand on him. He would wait until Chris least suspected before striking.

His brief fling with Chelsea had been eating away at his insides like a cancer ever since the night it had happened. Maggie had begun sensing something was wrong. He saw it in her eyes in the way she looked at him, and he supposed she wondered what she'd done wrong. He desperately wanted to come clean to her and plead for her forgiveness. But he was a coward. She would leave him for his indiscretion and she'd have every right to. He couldn't bear life without her.

He had hoped in time things would just return to normal and they would marry and he could put the affair with Chelsea behind him. Chelsea would be out of his life for good.

Instead, he found it progressively more difficult to live with his dishonesty, and his tormented soul wouldn't allow him to eat or sleep. He'd wake up in a cold sweat worried that Maggie would find out. Every day he tiptoed around her, wondering if she knew or when she would find out the truth. He became moody, and instead of turning to the woman he truly loved, unburdening his soul, and begging for her forgiveness, he distanced himself from her.

He began making up excuses for not spending the night, as much as he longed to hold her and erase that night with Chelsea from his mind. His one night of betrayal continued to haunt his thoughts day and night. He'd broken the trust he so cherished with Maggie. How could he touch her now after his infidelity? He'd dreamed of the day they'd start a family of their own, but now that could never be. He was trapped and there was no way out.

Chelsea was expecting his child, had insisted he move in with her and take responsibility for their unborn child. He felt like scum. He didn't have the decency to tell Maggie he was moving in with Chelsea. How could he tell her? What could he possibly say that would make his unfaithfulness easier for her to bear? She would never believe it was only a one-night stand. He couldn't stomach witnessing the pain and distrust that her eyes would hold for him. What would it do to her when she learned he was expecting a child with Chelsea, a child he had so desperately wanted to give her? A child she so desperately ached for? "God, what have I done?" he moaned.

CHAPTER THREE

Maggie's dark mood stayed with her as she cleared the table and put the few dishes in the sink. She stared at the silent phone, rechecking the answering machine, then poured another cup of coffee and carried it to the tiny living room. She didn't know whether she should be angry or hurt, but she wouldn't bring herself to call his apartment, not this time. She was tired, and suddenly she felt very used. Was she only a place to sleep over when he was horny? She assumed he would have made some sort of permanent commitment to her by now. After all, they'd been seeing one another for over two years, but lately every time she brought up the subject of solidifying their relationship, he had an excuse.

A couple of months ago, he was the one who'd implied he wanted to marry her. Or did he bring up the topic just to pacify her? She didn't know what to think anymore. The last time she'd mentioned his lack of interest in her, they'd gotten into an argument and he'd stormed out of the trailer in a huff,

25

not returning until the following night. Should she have given her trust to him? God knew how many times in her life she had given her trust too quickly only to have her heart ripped out, and then been abandoned to wallow in her pain and torment. She believed Chris was different. She'd given her heart and soul completely to him, and she didn't know how she'd get through it if he ever hurt her. She couldn't face that pain again.

She'd made a vow five years ago to never let a man do to her again what her ex-lover Jerry had done to her. She'd had everything then — prestige, power, and a beautiful home fully paid for — and was quickly rising to the top in the corporate world. She'd fulfilled her self-imposed quest to be successful by the time she was thirty. She was a young, rising, corporate executive until Jerry Wilder, a handsome young charmer, new in her department, set his sights on her and wouldn't be vanquished until she agreed to go out with him. Reluctantly she'd agreed, never imagining she'd be making the worst mistake of her life. She'd given her trust and heart to him, never perceiving that the corporate information she shared with him was secretly being used against her and her company. They'd talked about marriage and children. She was head over heels in love with him and assumed he'd felt the same way about her, but he'd only used her for the information she naively provided. She'd been too blinded by love to see what was happening right under her own nose.

Six months later he was gone, not only leaving her brokenhearted, but her personal and business life in shambles. After six months in prison, the short sentence, due to the work of a team of the best lawyers money could buy, she reentered the world to find everything she had once possessed gone. Jerry had fled the country when she was indicted, and throughout the ensuing trial it was learned that this wasn't his first scam. He'd made a practice of it, and he was good at seducing women. He had no remorse for the destruction he left behind. He was a player, and unfortunately, Maggie had been an easy target. She bitterly remembered her last night with Jerry and how their lovemaking had been more intense and sensual than usual. He'd been almost insatiable, and she had matched his passion, secure in the knowledge that together they would be as inflamed in the corporate world as they were together in bed.

It hadn't been uncomplicated putting her life back together. The lawyers' fees had taken most of her savings, meaning she could no longer afford the upkeep on her home or to live the lavish lifestyle she'd become accustomed to. She had enjoyed the wealthy status. She cried the day the For Sale sign was placed in the front lawn of her sprawling home, declaring to never again trust another man for as long as she lived.

She pounded the pavement day in and day out visiting every corporation head she'd even had a passing acquaintance with. She endured meetings, conferences, and lunches, but the outcome was always the same, even though no one had the guts to come right out and tell her they didn't trust her. But she knew it just the same. She saw it in their eyes as they quickly averted her own. It didn't matter to them that her innocence had been proven. She'd still shared corporate secrets, she was a risk they weren't willing to take. She'd been the most trusted executive in her company and she was the last person on earth anyone would have accused of leaking information, even if it were to a colleague in her own corporation. She was finished in the corporate world. Even though she knew her career was washed up, she refused to give up until she knocked on every last door.

After a year of trying to secure a position and her assets down to a few thousand dollars, she resigned herself to the fact that her career in the high-powered corporate world was definitely over. She'd have to start at the bottom of the ladder and try to work her way up again, but no one would even give her a second glance, let alone trust her to step inside that world again. People she'd once thought were good friends, even some she had helped to get where they were now, shunned her, and instead of offering her empathy, they looked at her as though she were plagued with an incurable disease, but she was determined to hold her head high. She wouldn't be beaten down by this misfortune. She'd done nothing wrong. The only mistake she'd made was allowing herself to fall in love with a cold-hearted fiend who walked around in the guise of a man seducing and destroying lives to enrich his own. He was a man without a conscience.

She knew her career couldn't be resurrected so she swallowed her pride, packed up her few remaining possessions, and moved to the poorer side of the city, the side she'd ignored and even turned her back on for the last ten years. Now she found herself needing to find acceptance here. She located an inexpensive trailer for rent and quickly put down the first and last month's rent on it. She shuddered thinking of living in the rundown home, but knew with some elbow grease she could brighten it up and make it cozy. Next, she set out on her search for a job, anything at this point would do, but she soon realized that she had to set her sights even lower than she'd thought when she couldn't even secure a job as a clerk or typist. She tired of the stern eyes peering at her as her resume was quickly tossed aside. She'd left out her position as a corporate executive, but just the same, her name and face had become familiar, making the interviewers look questionably and uncomfortably at her.

One day after a particularly discouraging interview she thought she'd aced but was turned down for, she happened into Tom's Diner for a cup of coffee. She'd been pounding the pavement all day and she was tired and dispirited. She wearily plopped down into a worn booth, ordered her coffee, and sat staring into her cup. She slipped her shoes from her aching, blistered feet. Tears of frustration slowly seeped from her eyes splattering onto her cheeks.

A soft-spoken voice close to her ear asking if she was okay caused her to turn with a start. She looked at the owner of the friendly voice. That was her first meeting with Tom Morgan. He introduced himself telling her he owned the diner. He sat down across from her, even though she hadn't invited him to do so. She soon discovered the affability in his eyes was genuine, and it wasn't long before she found herself pouring out her heart to him. She knew he wouldn't be able to help her, but it felt good to finally find someone who would listen to her without passing judgment. She was surprised when he offered her a job on the spot, promising only minimum wage and tips, but to Maggie it was like being offered the world and she graciously accepted it.

In time, she found herself becoming accustomed to not having all the monetary trappings of the world and settled into her position of the working poor. She quickly learned that being a waitress was hard and demanding work, but at the end of her shift, she had a satisfied feeling. She would survive. Her financial life would never be the same nor would her heart, but she would live through it. A door had opened just when she'd sunk to her lowest. She began to enjoy the slower pace of her life. Every evening she poured whatever energy hadn't been sapped during the day into fixing up her home. She was amazed at what a few coats of paint, pictures on the walls, and carpeting on the floor did to the place. With every paycheck she saved a little bit, and in the weeks when the tips were especially good, more went into her savings account. The day finally came when she had enough money to purchase new furnishings.

She gently warded off any questions from the inquisitive, who occasionally recognized her face from the newspapers or TV, and in time the curiosity wore off and she and her regular customers built a rapport with one another. She was changing from the woman she had once been. She slowly removed the shackles of her former self. Things she used to take for granted she now embraced—cherishing a beautiful sunset or the first flowers in spring. Now, instead of rushing everywhere with a quick nod of her head as greeting, she took the time for friendly conversation with others. She began to find peace within herself; a peace she'd never before known. She was finally getting to know herself, and she liked the calmer person she had become.

Her former way of living felt like it really hadn't been hers, but someone else's life. That person was a stranger to her now, and she was only reminded of what she'd once been when Brant Evans would make snide remarks about her past. He never came right out and said anything directly to her, but it was the roundabout way he commented on the financial state of the corporate company she'd once been a part of that let her know he would never let her forget. Aside from her unpleasant encounters with Brant, she found herself enjoying her work at the diner. She didn't miss the corporate meetings or phony camaraderie where every executive was planning how to screw the other.

She enjoyed her newfound freedom and would have continued on that way at peace and contented with herself and satisfied with her new life forever, but Chris Jacoby walked into her life one day, and as hard as she tried to resist, she found herself being swept into his world. She unlocked her heart to all he had to offer. She poured out her past to him, and he never batted an eye. He assured her repeatedly that he loved her for who she was now and that driven person she'd once been didn't exist any longer as far as he was concerned.

Now she was right back where she started from, emotionally anyway. The signs were all there, and she needed to prepare herself for another emotional upheaval. She blinked back hot tears as she finished her coffee, then set the cup in the sink and turned off the light. She walked to the small bedroom and slipped into her empty bed pulling the covers to her chin. Rain pounded against the windows, and loneliness seeped through her. She sighed. It would have been such a romantic night lying next to Chris's muscular body, safely snuggled in the crook of his arm. That was how it used to be.

How naïve she had been to have once thought she could take on the whole world as long as he was by her side. She was angry with herself for letting another man steal her heart after what Jerry Wilder had done to her. Her heart didn't want to believe that Chris might be with another woman, but her mind forced her to face that strong possibility. He wouldn't come right out and tell her because he knew she couldn't take the betrayal. She had told him countless times that her heart couldn't stand to be broken again, and if she lost trust in another human being, she didn't know if she'd ever trust again.

No, he wouldn't be able to look into her eyes knowing the pain that would be evident there, so he naturally took the safe way out. She concluded that he opted to stay away from her as much as possible until she figured out for herself what had really taken place. Her mind swam with possible, and hopeful on her part, reasons for Chris's aloofness, but the only logical conclusion was another woman. Tears formed behind her tightly closed eyelids as the pain in her chest intensified. She tossed and turned before falling into a fitful slumber shortly before dawn.

CHAPTER FOUR

Maggie wiped down the counter, watching as Janna purposefully made her way over to her. Heads turned as Janna walked, her hips gently swaying just enough to tease them into giving her their full attention. Maggie saw the way men looked at Janna, a way much differently than they looked at her. She knew she was attractive in her own right, but in a reserved sort of way. She hoped that as she aged she would become one of those women people said matured well and held their beauty.

She speculated how Janna would look when her youthful beauty faded away. Would a bitter old woman be left in her place when that day came? Men drooled over Janna, but never touched. Brant would destroy any man who came too close no matter how much Janna flirted. She was his personal trophy. Watching Janna, one quickly sensed by the gentle sway of her hips, plunging neckline showing ample cleavage, and the teasing smile that came from her puckered full lips, that she relished the attention she drew just as much as Brant relished the envy of other men.

"Hi, Maggie," Janna said with a wide smile, carefully perching herself atop a stool making sure she didn't wrinkle her expensive skirt.

Maggie eyed her sharply. She had to be up to something. It was unusual for her to stop in the diner without Brant glued to her side. In fact, it was unusual for Janna to visit this side of town unless she was visiting her friend Chelsea Howard. Janna had mentioned Chelsea a few times in previous conversations, and even though Maggie had been surprised that Janna associated with anyone from this section of the city, she never questioned the relationship. It was none of her business, and truthfully she didn't care. "What can I get you, Janna?" she asked in a clipped tone of voice.

If Janna had noticed the icy tone of Maggie's voice, she didn't let on. Impulsively she grabbed Maggie's hand giving it a gentle squeeze. The gesture startled Maggie. Janna was not one to offer anyone any type of kindness unless it benefited her own personal needs.

"I'm sorry about Chris," Janna whispered.

"Chris?" Her forehead furrowed.

Janna shot her a quizzical look. "Yes, Maggie. Now I understand why you were hesitant to accept my dinner invitation yesterday."

Maggie warily raised an eyebrow. "Janna, I honestly have no idea what you're talking about. I haven't even told Chris about your invitation yet."

"Oh, Maggie. I thought you knew." Her hand dramatically flew to her mouth as her eyes nervously flitted back and forth.

Maggie rolled her eyes. "Obviously I don't, so why

don't you fill me in?" she asked impatiently as she continued wiping the counter.

"Do you have time? Can we talk privately somewhere for a few minutes?" she asked looking around the sparsely populated diner.

She looked into Janna's crystal blue sparkling eyes trying to read something in them, but came up empty. "I doubt we'll be interrupted, it's slow right now. I can take a break."

Janna closed her eyes as she let out a mournful sigh. "This is going to hurt you, Maggie, and I wish there was some way to spare you this pain." Her voice sounded almost apologetic for what she hadn't yet said.

Maggie's patience was rapidly disappearing. "Look, if you have something to say, just say it. I don't have time for drama queen theatrics." She put the sponge under the counter then stood with hands on hips to face her antagonist.

"Is there somewhere we can go to speak privately? I don't want to talk here, Maggie." She glanced around at the few customers.

She shook her head. "We can talk here. Can I get you some coffee or anything?"

"No, thank you." She twisted the handle of her handbag. "I don't know how to break the news to you."

"Janna, just come out with it," Maggie snapped. "I told you I don't have the time or the patience for your silly games today."

The younger woman sighed again. "I suppose since there really is no easy way to say this, I should just come right on out and tell you."

"Please do."

She hesitated for a moment. "Chris moved in with Chelsea last night." Her eyes met Maggie's. "You know Chelsea Howard?"

Maggie felt like she'd just been kicked in the stomach. Her face flushed as a tremor slowly wound its way through her body. She inhaled sharply as Janna's words slowly repeated themselves over and over in her mind. "I don't believe you," she spat out tightly, gripping the counter as blood rushed to her head making her temples pound loudly against her skull. Her legs weakened. She'd pass out at any moment as Janna's stinging words continued to echo repeatedly in her head, slowly fading in and out. She sucked in her breath.

"It's true, honey. I wish I didn't have to be the one to tell you," Janna said softly.

Maggie shook her head. "No. no. I don't believe you." She glared at Janna as tears swam in her eyes. "How can you be so cruel, Janna? What sick pleasure do you get out of hurting others?"

Janna placed a ring-burdened hand on Maggie's shoulder. "I'm sorry. Brant and I are both sorry. Please believe me. We thought you and Chris had something very special together, but—"

She removed Janna's hand from her shoulder. "How long have you known?" she demanded.

"Brant and I knew Chris and Chelsea were occasionally seeing one another for business purposes, but we honestly didn't know it had gotten intimate between them. We were as surprised as you now are when we heard the news."

"Don't patronize me, Janna. Isn't Chelsea your best friend, and isn't she working in the police department?"

She raised her eyebrows. "She's a go-fer. You know, just out of college trying to decide what she really wants to do with her life. She has a fascination for criminal law but doesn't want to study law. She wants to catch them, not defend them, so she's just taking some time to figure things out." She laughed weakly. "She never let on to me that she was interested in Chris."

"If she would have, what would you have said? Would you have told her that he and I have been in a relationship for the past two years?"

"Oh, Maggie, of course I would have. I'm shocked that Chris never told her about you. I never thought him to be the type of man he's obviously turned out to be."

"How did they meet?"

She shrugged. "I'm not sure."

"Tell me the truth," Maggie insisted. "You must know how they met."

She looked down at her hands, and then brought her eyes back up looking evenly at Maggie. "Chelsea needed some shelves built for her new apartment and Brant suggested Chris for the job."

"Why would he suggest Chris? Chris doesn't have time to build shelves. He's been working twelve-hour or more days on the construction site."

"I don't know. I suppose Brant assumed that Chris would be able to build them the way Chelsea wanted them since he used to do house remodeling years ago. Besides, a little extra money never hurts. Brant knows the winter is rough for Chris."

"How long ago was this?"

"I'm not sure. A couple of months, maybe more."

"Chris never mentioned the job to me."

She shrugged again. "It probably didn't seem like a big

deal to him at the time. I don't think Chris or Chelsea planned for anything to happen. I'm truly sorry, Maggie."

Maggie's eyes flashed. "Janna, I don't believe you're sorry at all. I think you knew all along and couldn't wait to drop this bombshell on me. You waited for the perfect time to spring it on me. You and Brant didn't know if I knew or not so you gave me that phony dinner invitation to feel me out." She rapidly blinked back the tears now threatening to fall. She'd be damned if she'd let Janna see her cry. She'd never give her the satisfaction. "You probably encouraged them," she hissed. "You and Brant are the cruelest people I've ever met. You two deserve each other." She shook her head in disgust. "Now get the hell out of here and leave me alone!"

"Maggie...Maggie, I can't leave you like this. Let's talk about it," Janna said, her voice filled with sympathy.

"No. I have nothing further to say to you, Janna. You and Brant are behind this, but let me tell you something," she said pointing a long slender finger in her face. "Someday you and Brant are going to push the wrong person, and then you'll both be sorry." Her voice shook uncontrollably.

Janna slid off the stool. "Is that a threat, Maggie?" Her voice took on a less friendly tone.

Maggie glared at her. "No, it's a promise."

"Fine." She pulled back her slim shoulders. "I was only trying to offer my support, but I'll go if you insist." She reached out to touch her arm, but Maggie backed away. "Suit yourself, but I was sincerely only trying to help." She clutched her handbag tightly to her chest and then swiftly turned on her heel.

Maggie watched Janna walk to the door amid the lustful stares of a few truck drivers, and then disappear outside. She quickly composed herself then walked to her boss's office noting the door was slightly ajar. "Tom, I need the rest of the day off," she called from the doorway.

He looked up from the stack of papers lying in front of him. "Are you sick?" he asked, concern in his voice.

"No...I don't know," she stammered. "I just need to take care of a few things."

He stood up scratching his head. "It's slow today, so I guess it'll be all right. Just let Shell know that if it picks up out there to come get me."

"I will. Thanks, Tom. I owe you one," she replied, masking the pain she felt.

"Hold on a minute, Maggie." He walked to the door, then opened it fully and stood in front of her, peering down at her with a questioning look in his eyes. "I heard what happened between you and Janna Evans. I wasn't eavesdropping," he quickly added. "Are you sure you're okay?"

"No, but I will be," she answered, pasting a smile on her face. "I have a few personal matters to take care of. It'll work out, Tom."

****

He watched her leave and then walked back to his desk. Something wasn't right. An uneasy feeling seeped through him. This was not like Maggie at all. Something had been troubling her for days, something so deep she couldn't share it with anyone. Now Janna had to come and lay this news on her. How much more could she endure? He scratched his head again.

He liked Maggie. He'd liked her the instant he'd first laid eyes on her. She'd come from a different world than him and Shelly and the regulars around here. Her world had been the same world that Brant and Janna Evans lived in. He gave

39

her a break because he saw the woman she was underneath. She was a warm, gentle, caring soul who'd gotten a bad rap. She wasn't afraid to start over, and he admired that quality in her. She'd proven what a good, decent, honest worker she was usually taking on way more than was expected of her.

He knew she'd been in prison before she'd even shared that part of her life with him, and he also knew she'd been set up and managed to survive devastating losses in both her personal and professional life. She was a survivor. There was something special about her, and it was almost as if he could see inside of her way down to that gentle soul she possessed. She couldn't hurt a fly as far as he was concerned. She had class, and that was the one thing she'd never lose no matter what life threw at her.

He picked up a toothpick and stuck it in the corner of his mouth. No, whatever was troubling her, she'd work it out. She knew she had her family right here in this diner to help get her through any difficulty. He'd come to think of her and Shelly as the daughters he never had, and he knew their feelings for him were mutual.

Shelly Burgess had been with him since the day she graduated from high school. Now divorced, with two children at the age of twenty-four, he'd become almost like another grandfather to the children. Maggie had appeared to be resigned to her self-imposed single life, but Chris Jacoby had ended that. He brought a sparkle to her eye and a lightness to her step that made it known to everyone that she'd found love again.

Tom prayed that nothing would take that love from Maggie. If anyone deserved to be happy and loved, it was Maggie Allen. She'd paid her dues, and it was time she got something back.

CHAPTER FIVE

Maggie sat on the stoop, her face propped in her hands. Janna's words echoed repeatedly in her mind until she thought she'd go crazy. She placed her hands over her face as the tears freely flowed, wetting her palms, sobs racking her body as the pain in her chest deepened, and her heart slowly broke, then shattered into a million pieces.

After a few minutes her sobbing slowly subsided. She took a ragged breath as she pondered her next move. She was afraid, but she had to confront Chris. She couldn't just let him disappear from her life without an explanation, but most of all she needed to prove Janna wrong. Janna had to be wrong. Chris wasn't the type of man to do something as underhanded and cruel as this.

She ran inside and grabbed the phone, then quickly put it back down. No, she had to see him in person. She wanted to see his expression face to face when she confronted him. He'd become angry with Janna and Brant's unfounded rumors and assure her that Janna was lying. He'd have an explanation for his aloofness, and they'd work everything out. She grabbed her car keys and hurried out of the trailer.

****

Twenty minutes later, she pulled up to the construction site. She jumped out of the car and shielded her eyes with her hand scanning the workers, looking for Chris. She spotted him with two coworkers, his back to her, appearing to be deep in conversation. Slowly she walked toward the men. One of the men spotted her and said something to Chris. He turned and looked in her direction. The men patted him on the back then left.

His anxiety was obvious as she neared. She took her time, almost enjoying his noticeable discomfort. It suddenly dawned on her that the questions she'd been prepared to ask him, she'd just received the answers to as his eyes shifted nervously. She wasn't going to receive the assurance that Janna was a liar. His eyes told her that Janna was telling the truth.

"Maggie, I'm surprised to see you," he said uneasily.

"Chris, we need to talk." Her eyes pleaded with his for an explanation. She saw the muscle in his jaw twitch, remembering how it always did that when he was troubled about something.

He shifted his weight from one foot to the other. "I was going to come by tonight. It's busy around here right now, and I was just finishing up my break." He painfully looked past her. "We can talk later, okay?"

The tortured look she glimpsed in his eyes as they briefly met hers melted her heart. She didn't understand the pain he was in, and if it was caused because of hurting her, then why was he doing it? It didn't make sense. Nothing made sense anymore. A strong urge to throw her arms around his neck and comfort him overtook her, but that would be inappropriate under the circumstances. "What's going on, Chris?" she asked in a controlled voice as she ached to be pulled into those strong arms now hanging limply at his sides. "You haven't called...you just disappeared."

He looked at the ground as the color drained from his face. "I...I don't know what to say," he stuttered.

"Please look at me, Chris. Tell me the truth...that's all I ask."

He shamefully turned his head trying to avoid her eyes. With a shaky hand, he removed his hard hat and ran his hand through his hair. "I...I never wanted to hurt you."

Her eyes penetrated his. "Why, Chris? What did I do?"

He shook his head. "Nothing. You didn't do anything. It was my fault. I should have told you." His voice was strained. "Everything was my own fault."

She peered into his tired eyes. His face was drawn and haggard. Stubble showed on his usually clean-shaven chin. His hair looked shaggy and in desperate need of a haircut. If this was what loving Chelsea was doing to him, then she didn't know how he'd ever survive.

She'd expected him to feel badly for what he'd done to her, but she hadn't expected to see him so unkempt and miserable-looking. Seeing him wounded like this, though, helped to ease her pain even if just a little. He clearly was as miserable as she was. It made even less sense to her.

"Janna Evans came by the diner." She surprised herself at how even she managed to keep her voice. Anger momentarily flashed in his eyes. "Is that why you still kept your apartment so you could carry on with Chelsea Howard?"

43

Her tone was still even and controlled, but she knew that at any given moment she could lose total control. Her insides were quivering uncontrollably.

His eyes drifted again to the ground. "We're living together," he answered in a raspy, almost inaudible voice.

Maggie's chest constricted as a lump formed in her throat almost choking her. Her heart as fragile as a fine crystal vase now shattered into a million pieces. The earth felt like it was swaying beneath her feet. There was so much she wanted to say. She needed to scream at him for bringing this intense pain upon her. She wanted to throw herself at him and force him to see what he would be missing without her. In desperation, she needed to reach that part of his heart that would remember their passionate lovemaking and how they had almost seemed to blend into one. He needed to remember all the plans they had made. But looking at him now, she knew it was useless. The damage was done, and there was no turning back. Even if there was, she would never accept his betrayal. She doubted she could ever find it in her heart to forgive him.

He had made his choice and without any regard for her left her crushed and broken. She wanted to lash out at him and hurt him as much as he had hurt her. No, she wouldn't let him see how weak she was. She would gather her strength to leave, and she would never look back. It was over...finished. She had to pull herself together and recognize the fact that she couldn't give him what she thought he needed, what she thought he wanted. She turned on her heel.

His trembling hand touched her shoulder reaching out to stop her. "Please, Maggie. I need to explain. You deserve to know the truth."

"No," she whispered as tears formed behind her heavy

eyelids. "I don't want to hear the details."

"It's not the way you think it is," he hoarsely whispered. "Please believe that."

She forced a contemptuous smile as she swallowed the throbbing lump in her throat. "That's the lamest excuse in the book. You couldn't even attempt to come up with something a little more original. Save your explanations and excuses for someone who cares," she said breaking from his tender grasp as the tears she wouldn't allow him to see spilled from her eyes, blurring her vision as she blindly stumbled to her car.

****

Later she walked around the trailer from room to room emptying the cabinets and closets of Chris's belongings. She located a cardboard box and packed his items into it. When she finished, she set the box out by the front door then picked up the telephone, slowly dialing his cell phone number. This was a call she didn't want to make but had to. Her life with Chris Jacoby was finished, final, and there was no turning back now.

Her heart broke again when she heard his deep, cheery voice encouraging her to leave a message. She quickly composed herself.

"Chris, it's Maggie. You can pick up your things anytime. They're in a box by the front door." She didn't bother to say good-bye. What was the point? This was their final good-bye and they both knew it.

She sank to her knees as hot, heavy tears began to fall. "Why?" she moaned, wrapping her arms around herself. "What have I done to deserve this? I loved you so much, Chris." She couldn't stop the crushing pain ripping through to her very soul leaving it stripped and vulnerable. She couldn't endure this agony again, but she had to get all of the emotions involving Chris Jacoby out of her system or she'd never survive life without him. If she could make it through the next few weeks, she would heal and learn to live day by day without him. Each day would become easier to bear as long as she didn't see him. She prayed that Brant and Janna wouldn't add to her pain by showing up at the diner with reports on his life. She didn't know how much more she could take without snapping.

After her passions were spent, she stiffly pulled herself to her feet wiping her moist swollen eyes. "I'm better off without him," she said aloud. She spotted a photo of him, sitting by the telephone. She must have overlooked it earlier in her haste to rid the trailer of his belongings. She picked it up and started to toss it into the garbage, when she remembered the frame had belonged to her grandmother. She removed Chris's photo from the frame. She stared at it for a few seconds then tore it in two. A feeling of fury unexpectedly overtook her, replacing her dull heartache. In a rage, she tore it repeatedly until there were just little pieces left. She frantically searched the trailer for every picture she could find of him, giving them the same fate. When her rage was spent, she tied up the trash bag and then took it outside to the garbage bin and watched as the bag slid down the chute and landed with a dull thud when it reached its destination.

"You're out of my life for good, Chris Jacoby."

She walked back inside the trailer, put the teakettle on, and washed her face while she waited for the water to boil. After she fixed herself a cup of tea, she sat in the dark on the sofa with the steaming cup clasped tightly in her hands.

Minutes later she saw headlights coming up the driveway reflected in the window. It was Chris. She didn't look. She instinctively knew it was him. She heard the truck door slam, then seconds later footsteps on the gravel walking toward the trailer. She would recognize his walk anywhere. She'd become accustomed to his everyday mannerisms, being so in love and in sync with everything that was a part of him. She doubted Chelsea would give him the attention she'd so willingly lavished on him. Had she devoted too much of herself to him, giving in to his every whim whether he'd asked her to or not? Had she grown weak and needy in his eyes instead of the strong and confident woman she had been at the onset of their relationship? Had she let herself be taken for granted? Is that how he now perceived her?

She heard him pick up the box and take it to the truck. The truck door slammed, but instead of driving away, the footsteps came back. He walked up the two steps and then lightly rapped at the door.

CHAPTER SIX

Maggie stayed hidden in the dark, silently forcing herself to keep from bolting to the door and shamelessly throwing herself into Chris's strong muscular arms, the arms she'd always felt so safe and secure in.

She sucked air into her lungs, holding it there for a few seconds before expelling it. No, she wouldn't make a fool of herself, nor would she let him make one of her. He called her name. A tear slid from her eye at the mournful tone of his voice.

"Please, Maggie," he pleaded. "I need to talk to you."

She stayed silent in the shadows of the darkened room as her heart split open once again, spilling out all the memories she'd shared with him. She watched the images dance by through watery eyes brimming at the edge. She forced herself to concentrate on his deceit. She couldn't weaken and give in to him, she had to keep strong no matter how much it pained her. She willed herself to stay in the darkness fighting a silent battle within her. In the end, her firm resolve won out. She wouldn't give in. Never again would she allow her heart to be broken.

Five minutes later she heard his footsteps heavily move away, then the truck door slammed and the engine started. She wanted to leap out of her chair and go after him, but instead she sat and watched as though in a trance as the headlights grew dimmer and dimmer, until finally they were lost in the murky night, joining other vehicles speeding down the lonely highway.

He was gone from her for good now. She knew it was for her own good, but right now all she could think about was how much it hurt. The pain would last a long time. She didn't want to go through it again, but she had to. When you loved someone as totally and unconditionally as she had loved Chris, it was inevitable. She would ride out the pain and pray for the day when it didn't hurt anymore. That day would eventually come, but until it did, she would suffer her loss, which her heart likened to a death. Numbness overtook her, and even though the night was warm, she felt a chill that went straight to her bones. She grabbed an afghan and wrapped herself in it drawing her knees to her chin.

She was mentally drained, knowing she'd just lost the battle. Janna and Brant were the victors. They'd defeated her and were probably sitting in their fancy new home this very moment laughing and gloating at the latest blow life had dealt her. She didn't know how she would survive. She was tired of trying, tired of always losing out on the things she most desired. Mostly she was tired of always having to struggle just to find a little happiness. Yes, it was a difficult struggle just to survive the blows of life. That's all life had ever been to her, a game of survival. Her father never believed she'd amount to much no matter what her successes were, and it had only made her work harder.

She felt the need to constantly prove herself to everyone she met. That was her survival. Was it like that with everyone? Everyone had his or her own type of survival to deal with. With Shelly, it was providing for her boys. With Tom, it was coping alone after the death of his beloved wife. Why was life so unbalanced? What was the purpose of being born just to suffer? She pondered her soul, searching for answers to her own questions as she sank into a gray depression.

After several minutes, without any sensible answers, she chased away her dark thoughts, willing herself to summon up the strength to go on without Chris. It might have been easier if only she had some clue as to why Brant and Janna despised her so. She couldn't recall ever doing anything to offend either of them to warrant their nasty actions, but then maybe that was the problem.

Everyone in town bowed down to the both of them, especially to Brant, that is, everyone except her. She and Chris had socialized a few times with them but had never considered them friends. They reminded her of the shallow acquaintances she'd left behind in the corporate world. She didn't want to socialize with anyone who would remind her of her painful past. She had never been afraid to stand up to Brant's staunch opinions about world events and his racist attitude. She was not willing to back down from her own convictions just to pacify Brant Evans. She refused to agree with him just to pump his ego even more than it was, as so many others tended to do.

Brant Evans hated a strong woman. It was obvious. Everyone who knew him even remotely soon found that out.

In his narrow viewpoint, a woman was made to stand behind her man with the understanding that whatever he said or did was right, and she should never question his motive. A man's opinion was all that mattered, and women had no worthy opinions of their own. A woman was to remain silent and only serve as an ornament to her man.

Maggie loathed his self-righteous attitude and cringed every time Janna enthusiastically applauded his chauvinistic words and actions. Maggie would never let him get the better of her and he knew it. He made a game out of trying to break her down. If an individual didn't bow down to him, he could make their life miserable, and he usually did without batting an eye. His power lay in those at the police department. He had his own personal group who would do anything he commanded. He had more enemies than friends, but that never seemed to bother him. Money and power were all he coveted in his life. He was a man with a chip on his shoulder believing the world owed him something. But he never came right out and said what and why he believed he was owed so much.

She took small consolation in the fact that someday he would meet his match and have nowhere to run and no one to turn to. He would get what was due him. Then his miserable life would come full circle and his victims would have their revenge. It had to happen that way or nothing would ever make sense.

Nevertheless, that still didn't excuse Chris's actions. If he'd truly loved her, he would have never put her through this monumental pain. Their love should have been strong enough to unite them against anything Brant Evans threw their way. The only conclusion she could draw was that he had never

51

really loved her at all. At least not in the same way she'd loved him and still did. Even Brant couldn't force anyone to stop loving someone. No, if she'd meant as much to him as he did to her, then not even Brant would have been able to destroy that love. Chris has gone to Chelsea Howard of his own free will. No one held a gun to his head and forced him to sleep with her. If he hadn't wanted to, then he wouldn't have. It was as simple as that. She had to accept that painful realization and not allow herself to make excuses for him. In her vulnerable state, it would be much too easy to make excuses for him.

She walked into the bathroom, removed her clothes, and then stepped into the shower as the too-hot water splashed down on her easing some of her icy numbness. She took a bar of soap and roughly scrubbed her body, trying to rub away any remembrance of Chris, but she couldn't and she knew she'd never be able to. He'd penetrated the part of her heart she'd vowed no one would ever touch again after Jerry Wilder had flattened it.

What was Chris doing right at this very moment? Was he thinking about her? Was he sorry for hurting her? She remembered the sensuous showers they'd taken together, and it brought a longing smile to her lips. His powerful kisses had caused her knees to grow weak as the scorching fire of desire swept through her making her barely able to wait for his throbbing cock to enter her as the water from the showerhead beat down on them. She'd beg and plead for more as she rode the waves of ecstasy until he'd pump everything he possessed into her.

Afterward, they'd hurry into bed and continue making love off and on all night. She'd never known a man so virile. Rainy nights were the most romantic. She'd light candles and place a bottle of wine in the bedroom, then dress in her sexiest lingerie and patiently wait for him and the passion she knew lay ahead.

Maybe he was taking a shower right now at this same exact moment in time and was remembering the showers they'd taken together. Or maybe he was taking a shower with Chelsea and making new memories, already having forgotten about her. That thought brought a sharp pain to her heart. Chelsea was half his age. She rubbed her skin harder. Chelsea could be his daughter, for God's sake. She wondered how Chelsea felt fucking a man old enough to be her father and how Chris felt fucking a woman young enough to be his daughter. Even though Chris was handsome and strapping for his forty-five years, the age difference would eventually come into play when Chris discovered there was more than sex that he needed out of a relationship. Chelsea was just a child, and her immature ways would soon get on his nerves. Maggie was sure of it. What could they possibly have in common? They were from two different generations.

Her disturbing thoughts brought a lump to her throat. In bed Chris was a master and could put men half his age to shame. Even someone as young and energetic as Chelsea would have no problem being satisfied by him. He was tender, compassionate, and made certain his partner was as satisfied as he was. If Chris couldn't satisfy Chelsea, Maggie doubted any man would be able to satisfy her.

She turned the water off, her body now fully warmed, dried herself, and then walked naked into her bedroom and slipped between the cool sheets. She lay there for a few minutes tossing and turning as the scent of Chris permeated her nostrils, and when she could no longer stand his smell still lingering in the bedroom, she got up tearing the sheets from the bed. She grabbed clean sheets from the closet, then walked to the living room and made herself a bed on the sofa. Minutes ticked by, then hours. Somewhere near dawn, exhaustion overtook her and she slept until the shrill ringing of her alarm clock woke her.

****

Chris couldn't bear looking into Maggie's eyes when she'd shown up on the work site. She'd surprised him, and all the things he'd wanted to say to her stayed locked inside of his heart. He'd hoped she'd let him into the trailer...if she'd just give him a few minutes and hear him out, but he didn't blame her for not wanting to see him again. She'd been severely hurt in the past and he'd vowed never to bring pain to her, and now he'd brought the worst kind to her. He refused to give up though. No matter what it took, he'd be with her again. He determinedly set his jaw. He'd find a way to make all of this up to her, even though neither of them would ever be able to forget his deception.

Every time he looked into Chelsea's devious eyes, he knew that she'd planned this all along with Brant. But God help him when he found out why, and he vowed he would find out. Still, he had to do the honorable thing with Chelsea or his reputation in town would be ruined. He'd be accused of taking advantage of a woman young enough to be his daughter, not that the town gossips wouldn't be wagging their tongues in disgust with the age difference anyway.

He needed to talk to Maggie, though. Dammit, he should have told her right away, what he'd done, but now it was too late. She'd have nothing to do with him. He needed to reach her somehow, some way. He'd make her listen. He ached to hold her again and feel secure and comforted in her love.

How could he have been so stupid? He'd never again touched Chelsea since that one night. Chelsea knew he didn't love her. He showed her no affection. Why did she want to live like this in a relationship that didn't involve love? She was pushing him for a quick marriage to save face, but he was stalling. He needed some answers and until he got some, not even Brant Evans was going to push him into this unwanted union.

He took the picture he always carried of Maggie from his wallet and stared at her beautiful smiling face for a few minutes and then slumped to the floor covering his face in his large hands as sobs racked his body.

CHAPTER SEVEN

Maggie hurried into the back door of the diner, threw her purse and keys into her locker, and proceeded to the sink where she began washing her hands.

"Feeling better?"

She turned to face her boss standing behind her. Concern was evident in his eyes. "Yes, thanks, Tom. I'll make up yesterday's hours."

"Not to worry, Maggie. You never ask for time off and you certainly deserve some." He stuffed his hands into his pockets. "You do the work of ten people around here."

"Flattery will get you everywhere," she replied with a wry smile turning her attention back to the sink. When he didn't give her a comeback, she half turned noting his somber expression. "Is something wrong?" she asked, drying her hands on a paper towel.

"Oh, no…no."

She studied him. "I think I know you well enough by

now to know when something's bothering you, Tom."

He shifted his weight from one foot then to the other. "It's Brant," he said uneasily.

"What about him?"

"He was in here earlier asking all sorts of questions about you."

"About me?" she said raising her eyebrows. "What kind of questions?"

He shrugged. "Mostly about how well I really know you. If I've ever seen any outbursts of your temper, if you've ever had a violent reaction...things like that."

She rolled her eyes. "That's ridiculous." She laughed.

"Yeah, that's what I told him." He shot her an anxious smile.

She shook her head. "Why do you think he would he be asking questions about me?"

"I don't know. It didn't make any sense to me either. When I asked him if you were in any trouble, he said 'not yet'." He let his breath out slowly. "Look, Maggie, if you've gotten yourself in a fix, let me help." His eyes searched hers. "I'm sure we can straighten things out with Brant."

"But I haven't done anything," she answered. "I swear. He's just up to his old tricks trying to scare me, and only God knows why."

Relief flooded his face. "I believe you." He patted her shoulder. "Just don't get Brant Evans on your bad side. You remember what he did to Joe Ramsey."

"I don't think I'll ever forget. The sad part is not being able to prove anything that would hold Brant responsible."

Tom nodded. "A man like Brant Evans should be looking over his shoulder all the time."

Maggie's eyes narrowed. "No, he doesn't need to. He has his wife's money and power to protect him. They own this city, Tom, them and all of their crooked friends. They do whatever they want, and his connections at the station gets them off. The whole damned police department is corrupt." She threw her hands up in exasperation. "Poor Joe Ramsey never did stand a chance. But you have to give him credit for not backing down from Brant."

"Joe was a good guy...never hurt a fly. It's a shame."

"It's more of a shame that nobody could do a damned thing about it."

"All I know is that when I lay my head down at night, I can sleep with a clear conscience."

"That's the difference between you and Brant, Tom. You have a conscience. Brant doesn't."

"I don't know how people like him exist." He shook his head back and forth. "Well, in any event, if you need any more time off, Maggie, you got it."

"Thanks, Tom." She took a large slab of bacon from the refrigerator and began slicing it. She was helping Tom with the cooking today and Shelly was working the counter. Both women would take care of the tables, but Shelly would do most of the waiting on customers. If they got too busy then Tom would also wait tables. She was glad for the break from counter duty. As much as she liked the tips and the friendly conversations with the patrons, her mind was too weighted down today to keep up her cheerful façade for the entire shift. She knew anything, a favorite song on the radio or someone wearing Chris's brand of aftershave or cologne, could start the flood of tears anew.

"I need six slices of bacon, extra crispy, Maggie," Shelly called to her.

"Okay," Maggie answered as she grabbed the slices and arranged the bacon on the grill.

"Maggie, you have a visitor," Shelly called again a few minutes later.

She frowned. "Tell whoever it is I'm busy right now, Shell." She carefully turned the bacon assuming that her visitor was Chris. She was definitely not in the mood to see him, and she knew if she stalled long enough he would undoubtedly get the hint and go away. Away was where she wanted him. After what he'd done to her, she had nothing more to say to him. Everything that needed to be said had been said. Why waste precious words on something that was over? And over it was. After a restless night of little sleep, she was more determined than ever to put Christopher Jacoby out of her mind and life forever.

He wasn't worth her time anymore, and she painfully came to the conclusion in the wee hours of the morning that he wasn't the man she thought him to be. That man was just a fantasy she'd invented to block her mind from seeing his shortcomings. This morning she'd awoken with a fresh lease on life. She would make it. It would take time to mend her broken heart, but mend she would. She was a survivor, like it or not, and she would prove to Chris that she was strong. But she also knew that if she stood face to face with him he could break her resolve down in an instant, and she couldn't let him. She had to will herself to remain strong. She would never forgive him for his betrayal. Maybe someday she would be able to see him without emotionally falling apart, but not yet. It was too soon. She needed to become familiar with not seeing him around.

"I don't have time to waste, Maggie," a deep voice

bellowed.

Startled, she looked up at the sound of the voice since the only people allowed in the kitchen behind the counter were she, Tom, and Shelly. "What do you want?" she asked staring coldly at the intruder.

He leaned against the doorjamb, his steely gray eyes boring into hers. "I think you know the answer to that," Brant answered evenly.

She shot him a sarcastic look. "I don't know what you're talking about." Her eyes shifted back to the grill.

Tom was quickly at her side. "Something I can do for you, Brant?" He looked squarely at the younger man as he walked with a swagger into the room. The door swung back and forth behind him.

Brant impatiently drummed his fingers on the worn work counter. "This is between Maggie and me, Tom. It's police business and truthfully none of your concern. Why don't you just get back to whatever it was you were doing?"

"Well, I'm sorry, Brant, but no one is allowed in the kitchen...for safety reasons, you understand," Tom apprehensively explained.

"This isn't a social call, Tom. I said it's police business."

Maggie's eyebrows rose as she looked quizzically at Tom then back at Brant seeing the fire burning in his eyes and his mouth drawn into a taught line. His jaw was firmly set. He looked like he was ready to explode. A chill ran up Maggie's spine. She'd seen that look on his face before, but now it was more intense and it frightened her.

Brant kept his eyes fixed on her. "I'll get to the point, Maggie."

"Please do," she said facing the grill and turning the bacon as she regained her composure. "I have a diner full of hungry customers waiting for breakfast." She kept her back to him.

"Could you stop that? I need to ask you some questions." His voice was sharp.

"Here, Maggie, let me take over." Tom took the tongs from her. "Do you want to use my office?"

"No," she said firmly turning to face her antagonist. "Whatever Brant has to say to me he can say in front of you."

"Are you sure, Maggie?" Brant kept his eyes fixed on her. "You might be sorry later that you didn't keep this between the two of us," — he paused for effect— "for now."

She rolled her eyes. "Tom's staying. Just get to the point, Brant."

"Whatever you prefer." He took a notepad from his pocket. "I have to ask you some questions about the threat you made to my wife, Janna Evans, yesterday afternoon."

"What?" Maggie's eyes grew wide. "You're crazy. I never threatened Janna." She laughed. "I don't believe this!"

"Did you or did you not insinuate that my wife and I were responsible for Christopher Jacoby leaving you for another woman?"

She placed her hands on her hips as she stood mockingly in front of him. The fear she'd felt just moments before quickly left her. "I didn't insinuate it, Brant, I said it. Since when does that warrant an investigation?" She glanced at Tom who was observing the standoff with one eyebrow cocked.

Brant's eyes narrowed into two black slits. "Did you tell her that she'd be sorry for what she'd done?"

"What? You're nuts!"

"I can take you in right now for threatening my wife's life, and don't think I haven't thought about it. The only

61

reason I didn't have you arrested last night was because Janna begged me not to. You should be on your hands and knees thanking her for that." He pointed a finger in her face. "But let me tell you something, if you so much as even look at my wife the wrong way, I'll haul your ass in so fast it'll make your head swim!"

"Now hold on a minute, Brant," Tom broke in. "You have no right to talk to Maggie like this. She has rights."

"Stay out of it, Tom." He glared at the older man. "You don't need to become involved in this. Maggie needs to learn that life goes on and she's not the first woman to have ever been dumped."

"You bastard!" Maggie spat out without thinking of the consequences.

"I should take you in right now," he said squaring his jaw.

She looked fiercely into his cold, heartless eyes. "Go ahead. I've done nothing wrong. And what happened between Chris and me is none of your business…oh, I should take that back," she said with a touch of sarcasm in her voice. "You, as usual, couldn't stand to see me happy, so you had to make sure you ruined my life."

"Now, Maggie, what reason would I possibly have?" He chuckled. "You need help. Have you considered seeing a shrink? I can recommend someone, or better yet, you can sign yourself into the state hospital. It appears to me that you're on the verge of a breakdown. A long rest may do you some good."

Her eyes flashed. "Janna came here yesterday just bursting at the seams to tell me about Chris, but you know what? I don't care. He's not worth it."

Brant smirked. "I really couldn't stand to see Chris

dating someone so beneath himself…white trash," he sneered. "And if you don't care, then why did you lash out at my wife?"

Maggie's body trembled and she opened her mouth, but before she could speak, Tom hastily grabbed her arm. "Let it go. He's not worth it. He's only trying to provoke you," he whispered close to her ear.

"What's that?" Brant asked moving toward them. "What'd you say, Tom?"

"Nothing, I was just calming Maggie."

"Well, you'd better continue." He put his notepad back into his pocket. "By the way, Maggie, I'll let you know whether my wife decides to press charges against you for making threats against her life. In the meantime, you'd better watch that temper of yours." He tipped his hat as he slowly made his way out of the kitchen through the diner and out the front door.

After Tom was certain that Brant was gone, he slammed his fist on the butcher-block table. "That son of a bitch! Someone has got to do something. He can't keep harassing people like this."

"But he will keep on, Tom. No one can stop him." She was thoughtful for a minute. "At least not yet."

He sighed dismally. "I'm awful sorry about you and Chris. Just remember that I'm always here for you if you need to talk or even if you don't want to talk about it."

She nodded. "That means a lot to me, Tom."

He put an arm around her, and she rested her head against his firm chest.

Tom Morgan was like a father to her. He was the kindest, gentlest man she had ever known. She couldn't let Brant hurt him, and she knew that if Tom defended her too much, that's exactly what Brant would do.

After Tom's heart attack six months ago, she'd noticed how he seemed to age almost overnight. His ruddy, full-faced complexion was gone. In its place were sallow, thin, sunk-in cheeks where his once robust cheeks had been. He tired easily and had lost the youthful bounce to his step. Now at the age of fifty-eight he had more silver in his hair than black. Before the heart attack, he'd only had a few wisps of gray.

"We'd better get back to work. Looks like Shelly's got her hands full," Maggie said, noticing the orders piling up on the wheel which had several slips from Shelly's order pad stuck to it.

Maggie's mind drifted through the rest of the morning as she worked the grill. She wouldn't let Brant Evans destroy her. How many lives had he already destroyed, and how many more was he destined to destroy? Her thoughts took her back to a year ago, back to Joe Ramsey.

Joe was one of her favorite customers. He had a warm, friendly smile and made it his personal goal to cheer anyone who was down in the dumps. He didn't have an enemy in the world. He was the type of person who put everyone at ease with his generous sense of humor and simple way of looking at things, which made him loved by everyone who had the good fortune to make his acquaintance. He was a hard worker, supporting his wife and three children with his two jobs driving a local delivery truck and working part-time in the steel mill on the edge of town. No matter how tired he was, though, he always took the time to listen to anyone's problems, offering little tidbits of his well-earned wisdom. He lived a peaceful, laid-back life totally devoted to his wife Eve and their children. His true joy in life was being a husband and father, and his satisfaction came from providing for them.

That was until last spring about this time. Maggie shuddered at the memory.

She'd been working the counter when she noticed Joe shuffling in, his face drawn and fatigued. She instantly knew something was terribly wrong. "Hi, Joe, I'll get your coffee." She set a steaming cup before him.

His hand shook as he raised the cup to his lips. He used his other hand to help steady the cup.

"Are you all right, Joe? Are you sick? Can I get you something?" He looked like he'd collapse at any minute. She was alarmed.

He set the cup down. "No," he hoarsely whispered. "I'm not sick."

"What's wrong, Joe?" She looked into his eyes. Instead of the usual sparkle and gleam, they were now vacant, but worse was the sadness in them…a lost look that made Maggie want to lash out at whoever had taken the spark from this wonderful human being.

She'd never seen him like this before and it upset her. This was not the Joe Ramsey she knew. Something horrible must have happened for him to be in this condition. "Should I call Eve?"

"*No*," he emphasized raising a trembling hand. "I'll be fine."

A tormented look came into his eyes at the mention of his wife. "Did something happen to Eve or one of the kids?"

He numbly nodded as he clasped his large hands around the coffee cup, holding on as though he were holding on for dear life.

Her heartbeat quickened. "What's happened, Joe?" she asked in a wobbly voice. "Please tell me."

He looked at her with blurry eyes and then pulled a crumpled paper from his pocket. "Read this." His hands shook as he handed it to her.

Maggie smoothed the paper and began to read. When she finished, she handed the paper back to him. "Joe, this is ridiculous. Why would Eve believe you were running around on her?"

He shook his head as he slowly picked the cup up again.

"Who told her those lies?"

He let out a shallow breath. "Brant Evans."

"Brant? Why?"

He set his coffee cup down. "You remember a few months ago when my oldest boy Joey Jr. got arrested on a bogus drug charge and Brant roughed him up?"

"Yes, I remember."

"Well, Brant wasn't too happy about being called on the carpet, even though he and his cronies lied their way out of it."

Her eyes shifted. "No one thought it fair that Brant got away with it. But at least Joey was found innocent."

He sighed. "Well, it obviously wasn't enough for Brant. Not only did he get away with beating my son, but he vowed that he would someday get me for bringing trouble to his door."

"But you only did what anyone would do, Joe. Your son was violently assaulted. You had every right to file charges against Brant. Any parent in your place would have done the same thing. Brant had no right to touch your son, cop or not."

He looked down into his cup, then back up at her. Tears swam in his eyes. "But was fighting Brant worth losing my family over?"

"Surely Eve knows it was all lies. For Christ's sake, Joe, Eve knows what Brant's capable of. She's not blind to the things he's done. She should have seen that it was an act of revenge."

"That's what I thought." He gave her a desolate look. "She started questioning my every move and every dime I brought in or spent. Things got strained between us till we were barely speaking to each other." A tear slid from his eye. "In her place I'm not so sure that I would have believed me either."

Maggie patted his hand. "I'm sure she'll come to her senses, Joe. Just give her a couple of days and she'll be back."

He shook his head again. "I don't think so. We've been married over twenty years and she doesn't trust me. It'll never be the same because she'll always carry that doubt in the back of her mind."

"She knows how hard you work to support your family. She'll remember that and eventually realize that you're telling the truth."

He laughed dryly. "No, I held back some of the money. It was a surprise for her, but she'll never believe that now."

"Tell her now, Joe. It's worth a shot."

"I can't." He blinked hard as a visible shudder tore through him.

"Why not?"

"It doesn't matter anymore."

"Come on, Joe, give her a call and explain it to her."

"It's worse than that, Maggie," he replied in a ragged breath.

"What do you mean?"

"Some woman came to the house while I was at work.

She claimed she was returning a shirt I'd supposedly left at her apartment. She acted surprised that Eve was my wife and proceeded to tell Eve how she wouldn't have gotten involved with me if she'd known I was married."

"This is getting crazier by the minute, Joe. Who is this woman and how'd she get your shirt?"

"I have no idea who she is. She wouldn't give her name. As far as the shirt, though, I always have a couple of clean ones in the truck so I can change between jobs. Anyone could have taken one out. I rarely lock the truck." He shot her a painful smile. "There's never anything worth stealing in it. But the woman must have been convincing because Eve wouldn't listen to a word I said in my defense. I told her I would confront anyone with these lies, but she said the woman would have no reason to come over to cause us trouble. What would be her purpose?"

Maggie frowned. "We have to figure this out. None of it makes any sense."

He looked into her eyes. "It didn't make sense to me either until this morning."

She looked skeptically at him. "What happened this morning?"

"Brant pulled me over for a routine spot check. At least that was his excuse. He told me if I went right home I would find a big surprise waiting for me." He wrung his hands. "I ignored him and started to drive away when he said, "Paybacks are hell, Joe. Give Joey my regards.""

"That bastard! Joe, certainly Eve has to know it was all a setup. Come on. I'll talk to her if it'll help," she urged.

His chin trembled. "No. If she wants to believe that about me after all we've been through, then it's just not worth it."

"What happened when you got home?"

He blinked. "I found this note. She was gone. Everything was gone. It was like she had the move planned."

"Joe, why didn't you tell someone before now what was going on? Maybe we could have helped."

"I couldn't...you know me, Maggie. I've always been happy, carefree Joe Ramsey. Always listening, never confiding." He lowered his eyes and stared into his coffee cup. "Besides, I thought maybe I could convince Eve that I'd done nothing wrong. After all, in all the years we've been together there's never been any dishonesty or mistrust between us. I was hoping and praying every day that she'd know I wasn't capable of cheating on her, nor did I ever have the desire to. I figured in time maybe she'd come to her senses." He swallowed hard. "She's my heart and soul. When she left, she took a part of me with her."

The gut-wrenching pain he felt was etched on his face. She patted his shoulder. "God, Joe. I still wish you had said something. You don't always have to be the one everyone else leans on all the time. It's all right for you to do some of the leaning once in a while, you know." Tears stung her eyes. "Let me get you some fresh coffee."

He held his hand up palm facing her. "No...no, I think I'll just go home and try to figure things out." He slid off the stool.

He stood before her, his shoulders slouched as though he were carrying the weight of the world on them. And right now he was, Maggie sadly thought.

"You know something, Maggie? Eve was the only woman I ever loved, and I'm not ashamed to admit this, but she was the only woman I ever made love to or cared to make love to. She was always woman enough for me."

Maggie felt the heaviness of Joe's burden as she watched him lumber to the door. Her heart broke for him.

Joe Ramsey's body was found the next morning. A bullet had torn away most of his face. Beside his cold body was a blood-splattered letter addressed to his wife and a set of car keys. The letter explained how he had taken some money from each paycheck for the past few months to get her a badly needed car. It was to be a surprise for their twenty-first wedding anniversary.

"Maggie, I need two burgers medium," Shelly called. "Hey, you all right?"

Maggie came back to the present. "Yeah, I was just thinking about Joe Ramsey."

"It's almost a year now, huh?" Shelly's brows knitted together.

She nodded. "A year the end of this month."

"He was one of the nicest people I've ever met. There will never be another man like him. I miss him," Shelly quietly said.

Maggie nodded. "I know. We all do."

"Eve isn't the same. It's like a light has gone out in her life."

"I think she's going to blame herself for his death for the rest of her life."

"If she'd only believed him. It's a shame."

"I'm sure that thought runs through her mind every day. That and the realization that Brant set Joe up and she fell for it," Maggie said. "It's got to be rough, and I'm sure guilt must be eating her alive for ever doubting Joe."

"It's not fair that what Brant did couldn't be proven though."

70

"Brant always makes sure his tracks are covered, but someday he'll slip up. Someday someone's going to sneak up on him when he least expects it. He'll get his due."

Tom stood leaning against the butcher-block table listening to the conversation. "Hey, Mag, your shift is almost over. Let me grill those burgers," he offered.

She turned and flashed him a bright smile. "No, I'll do it. I'm in no hurry to get home."

He eyed her carefully as though he were reading her thoughts. "Brant's a dangerous man, Maggie. He plays by his own rules. He's not a man who likes to lose. Just be careful."

"I will, Tom."

Chapter Eight

Brant pulled a file from the safe. "Very soon it's all mine." He grinned. "The way Nick talked, it's even more than I thought."

"Did he give you a clue as to how much?"

"No. He just said that he had some information to go along with it. Knowing my father, he probably has another ridiculous stipulation like he did with the age."

Janna touched his shoulder. "Honey, you deserve it."

His eyes gleamed. "Yes, I do. That bastard put my mother through hell with all of his affairs. I remember sitting with her night after night while she paced the floors waiting for him to come home."

She ran her fingers through his hair. "You were a wonderful son to your mother and are a wonderful husband to me."

He squeezed her hand. "Everything that I am is because of you. You're my inspiration. I was only half a man until I met you. You make me strive to be the best, because only my best is what you deserve." He kissed her cheek.

She grabbed his hand. "I'd love to take the credit, but honey, you are a driven man and I know you'd be a success with or without me by your side." She smiled. "That's what I love so much about you, Brant. I never have to doubt your love for me. Before we met, I used to worry if I'd ever meet a man who would love me for myself and not just for my money." Her eyes twinkled. "Then you came into my life and gave me your sweet and pure love."

He caressed her soft skin. "Your money has never mattered to me. It's always been just you I wanted." He smiled. "Besides, honey, I knew I'd eventually be getting my inheritance. And even though it's probably not going to be enough to make me rich, it should be enough for a start in that direction with the right investments. I want to give you so much!"

"Your love is all I've ever wanted, Brant." She frowned. "Isn't it odd that your father put such a stringent age restriction on the inheritance?"

He shrugged. "Not if you knew him. My mother signed a pre-nup when she married him, and the will had a provision preventing her from contesting it. He'd left her barely enough to meet her monthly expenses. He was a miserable man and making me wait for the inheritance was his way of rubbing salt in the wound." He scowled. "He's probably laughing his ass off right now wherever he is."

"The restriction on the money just seems strange, that's all."

"I told you he was nothing but a rotten bastard. It was his way of having control over my life all these years." He looked into her eyes. "Believe me, you didn't miss anything by not knowing that man. Our future children are better off with him dead than alive. He would have only made their lives as miserable as he did mine," he bitterly retorted.

Her eyes brightened at the mention of future children. She couldn't wait for the day she became pregnant. "Our children will have so much love from both of us that they'll never know what an unhappy day is."

He flashed her a wide smile. "You know I wanted to sign a prenuptial agreement just to make certain you know how much I love you and not your money. And also so your friends would know I wasn't a gold digger."

"I know, and that's why I wouldn't allow it. I already knew your love was true and it was me you wanted. Your offer to sign was all the proof I needed to dispel any doubts anyone may have had. None of my friends ever thought you were after my money in the first place though. If they had, then they wouldn't be my friends, now would they?"

He cupped her face in his large hands and tenderly kissed her full, pink lips. "We're going to have it all, Janna." He stuffed the file back into the safe. "Don't wait dinner for me tonight. I don't know how long my meeting with Nick Saunders will take. Then I have to go back to the station and I never know what I'll run into there. But I promise that tomorrow night we're going to go out on the town to celebrate."

"Okay, honey. Good luck with Nick."

****

Brant's jaw dropped. "What the hell are you talking about, Nick? This doesn't make any sense." Brant shifted in his seat glaring at the attorney.

Nick Saunders removed his glasses and peered at

Brant. "No one was to know about any of this until the day arrived that the money was to be disbursed."

You act like it's a multimillion-dollar estate, for Christ's sake. How much is it, a couple of million?"

"It's much more than you realize," he replied quietly.

Brant scowled. "Fine, so what's the catch? Just give me the check and your duty as administrator will be over," he impatiently said.

Nick looked squarely at Brant. "Only half the money goes to you, Brant." He put his glasses back on. "This is what I need to discuss with you. Your father left explicit instructions."

His eyes widened. "You mean to tell me that he left half to my mother after all? Why didn't the good-for-nothing bastard let her have it when she most needed it so she wouldn't have had to live so frugally? Why did he make her suffer? It's too late for her now, since she's dead," he sarcastically replied.

"Brant, you know as well as I do that your mother never lacked for anything, but no, the other half was not left to your mother." He shook his head. "I wish I didn't have to be the one to tell you this." He folded his hands and placed them on the desk. "If it weren't for my friendship with your father, I never would have agreed to be the one to do this."

Brant's eyes flared. "Drop the melodrama, Nick. Whom did my father leave the other half to?" He slammed his fist on the desk. "It's another woman, isn't it? Who's the whore?"

"It's not what you think, Brant, but yes, your father did leave half to a woman."

"I knew it! That scum is still rubbing his affairs in my face!"

Nick cleared his throat. "Your father left twenty million dollars to you and twenty million dollars to your sister."

Brant's breath caught in his throat. "My…my sister?" he croaked. "What the hell's going on here, Nick? You know I don't have a sister, dammit."

Nick's eyes dropped to the folder on his desk. He inhaled sharply. "You never knew about her, but you do have a sister, Brant."

"What the fuck's going on? Are you trying to put one over on me?" His nostrils flared. "My mother certainly would have mentioned it. Is it a half-sister? Was my father previously married?"

"Your mother never knew about the child. Your sister was raised by her biological mother and grew up assuming that the man who raised her was her biological father. She carried his name on her birth certificate and I'm not certain if he ever knew the child wasn't his."

Brant slowly shook his head back and forth. "If my father's name isn't on the birth certificate, then how do you know for certain that this woman is my father's child?"

He sighed. "There were actually two birth certificates. I have the original."

"You're telling me that my father paid someone off to keep his deception all these years? Is this supposed half-sister of mine's mother in on this deception? Did she know about the original birth certificate? Is she looking for money?"

"Your sister's mother is deceased, and she knew nothing about this. In a moment, I'll turn this folder over to you. It'll explain everything."

"Did my mother know my father had a bastard?"

"No, Brant, I already told you that she never knew. He went to great lengths to keep the truth hidden from her."

"How could you keep this secret all these years, Nick? You're supposed to be a trusted family friend. Where was your loyalty?"

"I think my loyalty speaks for itself, Brant. No one knows the truth except you and me."

"What about this woman who allegedly is my sister?"

"Her parents are dead, and she's never been told the truth. She knows nothing about the inheritance."

Brant's eyes brightened. "So why do we need to tell her? Just give me all the money and I'll make it worth your while." His eyes slanted. "Don't tell me that thought hasn't entered your mind. You're only human, and just think what you could do with this extra money," Brant enticed. "How much would it take for you to destroy these papers and keep your mouth shut?"

"I'm going to pretend I didn't hear that." He leaned his elbows on his desk. "Don't you even care that you have a sister, Brant? Don't you want to know anything about her?"

He shrugged. "Why should I? We didn't grow up together. I know nothing about her, and no, I don't care to. My father probably got one of his lowlife whores pregnant, and she's probably scum too."

"How can you jump to conclusions about someone you don't even know?"

He threw his hands up. "Okay, fine, then tell me who she is," he impatiently stated. "Who's my sister?"

He looked into Brant's cold, dark eyes. "It's Maggie Allen."

CHAPTER NINE

Janna patiently waited for Brant to return home with his news from the lawyer. Good or bad, she'd help him through. She always did. She knew he was counting on the inheritance, but God only knew why he needed it so desperately when she had more than enough money for the rest of their lives and beyond. She willingly shared all she had with him, but her money never seemed to be enough. His appetite was insatiable when it came to money. She assumed it had something to do with his male ego and the years after his father's death when he and his mother had struggled financially.

Brant Evans aspired to be the best in everything he set out to do, and he would never let anyone think that his successes in life had come from anyone but himself. He was a proud man, but she saw his dark side too. At times it frightened her and she felt as though she didn't know him at all. She was always greatly relieved that his violent outbursts weren't directed at her and pitied the poor souls they were directed at.

She slowly ran a brush through her silky hair. Her friends had never understood her sudden, almost suffocating, obsession with Brant. Many had warned her about his sinister side, but she refused to believe that he would ever be anything but warm, kind, and compassionate toward her. And that's how he'd been.

He'd eased right into her world as though he'd been born into wealth. In fact, many of her friends forgot that he hadn't been. His manners and dress were impeccable, and he was an intelligent businessman with an unquenchable appetite for new investments. She was both relieved and pleased that her friends warmly accepted him even when they found out that the Cedar Pines Police Department employed him. His lack of a wealthy social standing and the decision to keep his job didn't bother them, or her. Sometimes she suspected they even relished his employment if it could be used to their advantage, and she knew that on many occasions Brant was responsible for charges miraculously being dropped. That only endeared him more to them and made them quickly forget his dark, sinister side. Despite the fact that his power wasn't due to inherited wealth, his power lay in his employment and he wielded it at every opportunity for his own purposes.

She'd often thought he'd excel in a political career, but when she'd intimated it to him, he smiled but showed no real enthusiasm. After they were settled down and with a couple of children, she intended to talk to a couple of her friends and maybe together they could convince him to direct himself in that area.

Her friends had more readily accepted Chelsea knowing that Chelsea had come from a life of hard work and an ancestry with no illustrious heritage. They never assumed that she was just another project for Janna who had a knack for taking the lonely and downtrodden under her wing. Janna had immediately taken a liking to the girl envying Chelsea's freedom to be whom she chose to be. Janna knew that she herself was expected to play the role of pampered princess, so Chelsea was like a breath of fresh air when she breezed into Janna's stifling, sheltered life. Janna's friends came to accept and love Chelsea, seeing the positive effect she had on Janna's life, opening her up to new experiences and adventures.

Brant had also taken an immediate liking to Chelsea, and Janna surmised it had to do with the fact that they shared the same middle class upbringing. There was almost a kindred bonding between Brant and Chelsea. Janna never knew or understood the world they came from, a world of wanting and struggling for everything. She was grateful that she had been spared from that sort of existence. She doubted she had the constitution to survive such a hard life. The thought of it made her shudder. Hers had been filled with every advantage possible. She'd been abroad so many times that she'd lost count. If there was any drawback to her life, it was that she'd never gotten close to either of her parents. Her life revolved around servants and her much-adored nanny who'd been with her until her sixteenth birthday. She cried the day the elderly woman retired from their employ and mourned her passing two years later almost as much as she had her parents.

When she met Chelsea it was like a new world where she could, even if only for a while, drop the shackles of her wealth and step into the world of total freedom and wild abandon. Then she was just like any other young woman out for a good time where she didn't feel as though she were on display for the society papers. She'd never laughed so much or felt as liberated as she did when she and Chelsea were together.

Meeting Brant had brought more change to her life. He carried her into a world of excitement and romance she'd never known could exist between a man and a woman. The society boys she'd been accustomed to were stuffy and boring, so Brant Evans was like a breath of fresh spring air after a rainstorm. He truly had swept her off her feet just like in a romance novel. She smiled, remembering how poetic and beautiful his words had been when he was courting her. He loved her for who she was. Her sensibility, though, reminded her that her wealth didn't hurt, but Brant made her feel like she was the most important woman in the world. That was all that really mattered.

When Brant had introduced her to Chris Jacoby, she'd been surprised. She never would have taken them for friends. They didn't seem to have much in common, but Brant liked Chris, or at least that's what he told her on several occasions. Chris was a good man — one who could be trusted, and that type of man was far and few between in this day and age. Brant had become deeply disturbed when he discovered Chris was dating Maggie Allen. She didn't understand why that fact had upset him so, but then everything about Maggie Allen seemed to upset him. He'd followed her career in the papers, and Janna believed Maggie's success was what disturbed him the most. Maggie had come from nothing and with hard work and determination had made her way up the corporate ladder. She was no stranger to the media and her face had often appeared in magazines, TV, and the press.

Janna suspected that Brant was jealous because a woman had become so successful when in Brant's opinion, a woman had no right in the corporate world. He'd hooted and shouted with glee when Maggie's world crumbled. Janna had thought that would be the last she'd ever have to hear of Maggie Allen, but Brant wouldn't let go. After Maggie was released from prison, he made it a point to track her whereabouts. He was a man obsessed, and at times it alarmed Janna.

When Maggie began working at Tom's Diner, Brant made it a point to frequent the quaint establishment with Janna securely planted on his arm. When Chris Jacoby began dating Maggie, it ate away at Brant. He constantly made snide remarks about Maggie not being good enough for Chris. The tension between Maggie and Brant was unmistakable from the first moment they laid eyes on one another, but Brant suppressed his emotions insisting that Janna become friends with Maggie since Chris was a friend of his. Whenever Janna looked into Maggie's eyes as Maggie was looking at Brant, she saw the same contempt for Brant that was in his eyes for Maggie.

****

Brant nodded to Officer David Dennings. "I'll be making an arrest later this afternoon or early evening."

"Do you want me to assist?"

He sneered. "No, this one's all mine." He picked up the phone and impatiently drummed his fingers on the desktop as he waited for his call to be answered. When he heard the receiver pick up, he didn't give Janna a chance to speak. "I need you to get down to the station as soon as possible to file charges against Maggie Allen."

"Are you all right, Brant? What happened with Nick Saunders?"

"Just get down here and I'll see you later tonight and fill you in on everything." He hung up the phone and turned to Dennings. "When my wife gets here, take her statement. After she leaves, page me."

"Will do."

****

Janna made her way to Dennings' cluttered desk. "Hi, Dave, is Brant around? He asked me to come down."

Dennings quickly got to his feet and extended a hand to her. "Nice to see you again, Janna. No, Brant is out taking care of some business." He motioned to a chair. "Please have a seat. Brant would like me to take your statement about the threat Maggie Allen made on your life."

Janna frowned. "It's not as serious as Brant has made it out to be."

He leaned back in his chair carefully scrutinizing her. "Well, did Maggie Allen threaten your life or not?"

"She made a threat, but I think Brant has blown it out of proportion."

He thoughtfully rubbed his jaw. "I don't know about that, Janna. Every day threats are made and usually by seemingly normal, stable people no one would ever suspect possessed a violent bone in their bodies. Then the next thing you know there's a murder. No threat should ever be taken lightly."

"It's not as though she threatened to kill me or anything, Dave. Brant has built this up to be much more than it was, and I don't see the need to take it any further. He already talked to Maggie so I think he put a scare into her, and we can drop it. Quite frankly, I'm embarrassed that he's taken it this far."

"Let me ask you something, Janna. Why did you come down here if you had no intention of filing a statement?"

She narrowed her eyes. "I was hoping that I could discuss this with Brant."

Dennings tapped a pencil against the palm of his hand. "So you aren't going to press charges, then."

"How do you think Brant will take it if I decline?"

He snorted. "You know how Brant will take it. He's your husband, and you of all people should know how he reacts when things don't go his way."

"It doesn't feel right."

"It's your call, but remember, Maggie Allen did make a threat. And Brant loves you and is doing everything a man can do to protect the woman he loves."

Janna struggled with her conscience for a few seconds as Dennings' eyes examined her. She knew what he was thinking. She'd be a fool to not do what Brant wanted and expected her to do. Brant and his fellow officers were as thick as thieves. All Brant had to do was snap his fingers and they jumped to attention. But why? What did he lord over their heads that would put them fully under his command? That was the one thing about her husband she'd never been able to figure out.

"Well, are you going to give me a statement or not?" he impatiently asked. "I have a shitload of paperwork to get to."

Janna nodded. "Yes, I'll give you a statement."

CHAPTER TEN

Brant walked up the three stairs to the small entrance porch and knocked on Chelsea Howard's door. A few minutes later, she flung the door open, then seeing him, threw her arms around his neck.

He roughly disengaged himself from her. "What the hell are you doing? Someone might see."

"I'm sorry, baby," she cooed. "I'm just so happy to see you, that's all." She led him inside the stuffy apartment and over to the sofa. "I saw the doctor today. The baby is strong and healthy," she beamed. When he didn't respond, she pouted. "Don't you care about the baby?"

"Yeah, of course I do," he unenthusiastically replied.

"You don't act like it, honey."

"Well, right now we've got more urgent matters to discuss. When are you going to marry Jacoby? Time's running out and we've got to move fast before the old boy starts figuring things out. Sometimes he's smarter than we give him credit for."

"I don't think he will, Brant. We slept together, or so he thinks, so he assumes the baby is his. He hasn't even questioned paternity." She laughed. "He's old-fashioned. He'll do what's right and that means marrying me."

"I don't know," Brant said, thoughtfully scratching his jaw. "He might ask for a paternity test. After all, you're young and he might start to question who else you may have been with before or after him."

She shook her head. "No, I don't think so. He's too hung up on Maggie Allen to even think straight."

"All the more reason to worry," he reasoned.

Her eyes narrowed. "I don't understand."

He sighed disgustedly. "It doesn't take a genius to see what's right in front of your eyes. But since you apparently don't, then let me spell it out for you. If Chris is hung up on Maggie, then why in hell would he want to claim your child without question? If he does that, then he'll never have a chance with Maggie again. He's not stupid, and I think eventually once he gets the cobwebs out he'll realize that and want concrete proof that he fathered your child."

She bit her bottom lip. "What will we do if he does demand a paternity test?" she worriedly asked.

"It's not what we'll do, but what you'll do."

"It's not my entire responsibility, Brant. You can't put this all on me, not now in my condition."

He snorted. "Maybe that's something you should have thought about before you so willingly spread your legs."

****

Maggie threw her car keys on the coffee table, then removed her shoes and wiggled her toes. She was tired. Standing on her feet all day exhausted her, and now a sluggish drowsiness slowly wound its way through her body. She lay down on the sofa and closed her eyes knowing that sleep would soon come without much effort on her part. Her body screamed for rest. The phone rang, but she did not attempt to answer it. Her answering machine picked it up after four rings.

"Maggie, I need to talk to you."

Her eyes popped open and her heart pounded as she heard Chris's deep, pain-filled voice.

"I need to explain things to you. I know how much I've hurt you, and I'm suffering as much or even more if you can believe it." He paused. "Call me. Please?"

She got up, walked over to the answering machine, and pushed the erase button. "No, Chris, never again," she resolutely said.

She wouldn't be able to sleep now so she skimmed the day's mail and then popped a TV dinner into the microwave. She made a pot of coffee and paced back and forth while it brewed. She couldn't get Brant Evans or Joe Ramsey off her mind. It was overshadowing her, eating at her insides. How dare Brant threaten to arrest her? Her anger mounted.

A car pulled into her driveway. She didn't look, it had to be Chris. Seconds later, a loud knock sounded at the screen door. She ignored it, but the knocker grew persistent. Reluctantly she walked over to the door surprised to see Brant peering at her through the other side of the screen door.

"Open up, Maggie."

"What's the matter?"

"Just open the door." His voice was insistent.

"What's going on?" she demanded.

"I'm here to place you under arrest for threatening the life of Janna Evans."

"What? Give me a break." She smirked.

"Now, Maggie, you can make this easy or hard on yourself. It's your choice. You can come peacefully, or I can take you in by force." He glared at her as he tried to open the locked door.

She shook her head. "This is ridiculous, Brant. I never threatened your wife with bodily harm."

"Open the door!" He shoved it with his shoulder. "We can add resisting arrest to the charges if you'd like."

She saw the fire in his eyes. "Hold on a second." She slid the lock back.

He stepped into the kitchen. "Anyone else here?" He glanced around the room.

She eyed the handcuffs dangling from his hand. "No." She turned off the microwave and the coffeemaker. "This is a big mistake."

He grabbed her arms pulling them behind her as he handcuffed her.

"Come on, Brant. Don't you think you're taking this too far? I don't need those cuffs on me, for God's sake! I never threatened Janna and she knows it. Why are you really doing this to me?"

He ignored her. "You have the right to remain silent."

"You're going to pay for this, Brant," she hissed as he finished reading her rights and led her out of the trailer and into the waiting police car. The small crowd of neighbors that had gathered out of curiosity mortified her. Even though she had no more than a passing acquaintance with any of them, she was appalled as they continued staring at her as Brant drove down the driveway. Her face reddened with embarrassment.

Twenty minutes later, she found herself standing next to Brant at the Cedar Pines Police Station.

"Book her for attempted murder," Brant stated.

"This is ridiculous," Maggie explained to the booking

officer. "I want to make a phone call. I never made an attempt on anyone's life!"

The officer ignored her request. "You're going to be processed. I need to ask you a few questions first."

"Wait a minute! I demand my rights!"

Brant smirked at Officer Dennings. "She's been read her rights."

Maggie skeptically raised an eyebrow. "Now I don't claim to be an authority on the law, Officer Dennings, but I do know that I'm entitled to a phone call and legal counsel. I also know that I do not have to answer any of your questions without legal representation."

"After you're processed you can make a phone call," Dennings replied.

"I have rights!" she loudly repeated.

Brant placed his hands on the desk behind himself and leaned back as he carefully eyed her. "Now, Maggie, I hope you're not trying to imply that your civil rights have been violated. Because if you are, it's going to be very time-consuming and costly to prove, and I seriously doubt you have the money or other financial means to fight the Cedar Pines Police Department. You don't stand a chance, and I'm only telling you this to save you the time and trouble."

She whirled around glaring at him. "I'm not afraid to try. I'm not frightened of you, Brant. You can intimidate me all you want. You're not God, so quit trying to rule over everyone." Her eyes swept over him. "You want to break me for reasons that only you seem to know, but you can't. I know my rights," she emphatically stated.

He stared at her for a minute, his facial features hardening. "For someone who professes to know her rights, you seem to forget that it is against the law to threaten the life of another. It is my sworn duty as a peace officer to make certain that the individuals of this city are protected from you."

She scoffed. "I never threatened Janna, and you can't seem to get that through your head. Why she said I did is beyond my comprehension."

"It's not up to you or me to decide. That will be for a judge to determine." He glanced at Dennings. "Maybe you can convince her that it'll be easier on herself to plead guilty when she goes before the judge. Warren doesn't take too kindly to threats."

"Not on your life," she snapped. "I have nothing to hide, and I'll be damned if I'll plead guilty to something I never did."

Dennings scratched his head as he looked at Brant. "I guess we've got us a new prisoner. Don't get too many women in here," he said with a grin showing off his heavily tobacco-stained teeth. "Usually only hookers." He laughed. "Hard to say whom you'll be bedding down next to tonight. Some of them are mean and nasty."

Brant sneered. "Believe me, Maggie. Soon you'll find out that Chris Jacoby isn't worth all this trouble."

"This has nothing to do with Chris. This has to do with whatever vendetta you have against me."

His lips curved into a half-smile. "Jacoby and Chelsea plan to be married before the little one arrives."

Maggie's throat dried out. "What are you talking about?"

He raised his eyebrows. "Well, well, well. I guess you're the last to know. Chelsea is expecting. Chris is the proud papa-to-be. Maybe they'll invite you to the christening."

Her hands shook and she tightly clasped them together, her knuckles turning white as a stabbing pain shot through her heart shattering it into a million pieces.

Brant observed her. "It looks like this piece of news has come as quite a shock to you."

She knew he was enjoying her discomfort. She summoned up her resolve. "Whatever Chris does is no concern of mine." She tossed her head back. "Now, if I don't receive my phone call, then I will be filing charges for violation of my rights."

Brant laughed. "Always need to get the last word, don't you, Maggie?"

She fumed but kept silent.

He nodded to Officer Dennings. "Give her the phone call, then book her."

****

Chris sat in a booth at Tom's Diner chatting with a few patrons as he sipped his coffee. He caught Tom's eye and motioned him over.

Tom slid into the seat across from him. "Good to see you, Chris. It's been awhile. No offense, but you look like hell."

He ran a hand over his jaw. "If I look as bad as I feel, then I don't doubt it." He flashed a weak smile.

"We miss you around here, Chris."

He stared into his coffee cup. "Does Maggie miss me?" he asked hopefully. "Does she ever mention my name?"

Tom slowly exhaled. "You know that Maggie's like a daughter to me. She's hurting and I hate to see her suffering, but I don't get into her personal business unless she asks for my advice."

"You didn't answer my question."

He slowly shook his head. "She's hurting."

"I never wanted to hurt her. You have to believe me, Tom."

He was clenching his cup so tightly that Tom thought it

91

would shatter in Chris's large hands. "I never thought you did, Chris. It's none of my business what happened between the two of you, but my heart breaks seeing Maggie so heartbroken."

"I should have come clean to her, but I couldn't. I was a coward, and now it's too late." He looked up at Tom. "I—I need to talk to her."

Tom looked into the man's red-rimmed, blurry eyes. He wondered when the last time was that Chris had gotten a decent night's sleep. His eyes had deep, dark circles under them, and he looked like he'd lost an enormous amount of weight. "I wish you would have talked to her, Chris. It would have been better for her to hear it from you instead of Janna Evans."

Chris vehemently shook his head. "Janna had no right to tell Maggie anything. It wasn't her place."

"Whether she had the right or not isn't important at this point. What's important is that Maggie found out you were unfaithful and you moved in with another woman without so much as a word to her. Can you blame her for not wanting to talk to you? That was low, Chris, and not like you at all."

Chris's face reddened. "It was only one night with Chelsea, Tom. I swear! I only slept with her one time."

"One night too many," Tom firmly replied. "I can't justify what you did so please don't ask me to."

"I'm not asking you to, Tom. I just need to unburden myself to someone, and I've always trusted and respected your opinion. Please just hear my side of it," he pleaded.

Tom nodded. "I'm listening."

He swallowed hard. "I want Maggie back. I'll do anything to get her back. Just tell me what I can do. You see her every day, Tom. Tell me what to do!" he desperately implored.

"Chris, you can't just snap your fingers and fix what's happened. You hurt Maggie in the worst possible way a man can hurt a woman. You stepped out on her. Do you have any idea what that's done to her? I'm surprised she hasn't had a breakdown, but she's keeping herself together."

"God, I know," he choked. "But I need to try to make her understand. I'm nothing without her, Tom."

"Let me get you some more coffee, Chris." Tom held up Chris's coffee cup signaling to Shelly who promptly refilled Chris's cup and set a fresh one before Tom.

"It's nice to see you, Chris. Anything else?"

"No, thanks, Shelly. It's good to see you too."

"Why don't you get ready to close, Shell? I'll lock up tonight," Tom said.

Shelly nodded as she walked back to the counter.

"Am I keeping you from anything, Tom?" Chris asked.

"Just from another boring night in front of the TV." He rested his back against the booth.

"I don't know how my life got so screwed up. One minute I was the happiest man in the world, and the next the most miserable human being to walk the earth."

Tom picked up his coffee cup. "Sometimes we don't know how good we have it until it's gone. It's probably one of the hardest lessons we'll ever learn. And sometimes we just have to accept the fact that we can't undo what we've done."

"My life is meant to be with Maggie. I knew it from the minute we met. I can't go on for much longer without her. But she refuses to speak to me."

"You can't blame her for not wanting to talk to you, Chris. You made a fool out of her." He set his cup down. "No one can make Maggie talk to you. If she decides to, then it will have to be her decision and in her own good time."

"Could you talk to her for me, Tom?" he pleaded. "Just convince her to hear me out. If she gives me that chance, then if she never wants to see me or talk to me again, I promise to leave her alone."

Tom saw the hopelessness in the younger man's eyes and wished there was something he could say or do, but he knew there wasn't. Chris made his bed and now he had to lie in it. "It's not my place to do that, Chris. Especially after Brant's visit here."

His eyes widened. "What about Brant? What was he doing here?"

He cautiously eyeballed Chris. "He's out to make trouble, and it looks like Maggie is his current target."

Chris's jaw twitched. "She's never done anything to him. He's got to be stopped. Dammit, Tom, he's destroyed so many lives." His large fists clenched into two tight balls. "I swear if he hurts Maggie, I'll kill him. You can give him that warning from me."

"He'll keep on destroying lives until the day he dies, I'm afraid. That's what he does best—hurting others." He slowly shook his head back and forth. "But if he does anything to Maggie, I'm afraid when I'm done with him there'll be nothing left for you," he said matter-of-factly. "The best piece of advice I can give you, Chris, is to wait awhile before trying to contact Maggie again. The wounds are too raw right now and maybe in time she'll talk to you, but like I said, it has to be her own decision."

"Chelsea's having a baby," he blurted out in a strangled voice.

"What?" Tom's eyebrows shot up in shock. "Please tell me that I misheard what you just said, because if I didn't, then that puts a whole different slant on things." His lips drew tightly together.

Chris grabbed his arm. "Tom, please listen. It was only one night, for God's sake! I only slept with her one time"

"Last I knew, that's all it takes, Chris," he said sharply. "Under these circumstances, I think the best thing you can do is stay away from Maggie for good. This news will surely kill her."

"I have no proof that the baby is even mine."

"Have you been tested?"

"No."

Tom abruptly pulled himself to his feet and then extended his hand. "I wish you luck, Chris. The only piece of advice I have for you right now is to get tested. Find out one way or the other if Chelsea's baby is yours. Either way, though, don't count on Maggie wanting to talk to you for a long time…if ever."

****

Chris watched Tom shuffle to the counter, then finished his coffee and threw a couple of bills on the table before leaving.

He aimlessly drove around for half an hour. He spotted a vendor selling roses by the side of the road. He stopped and bought one, carefully placing it on the seat next to him. He drove to Maggie's trailer, gradually making his way up the driveway. Her darkened home reminded him of how darkened he felt inside. He wondered where she was tonight. She wasn't working. He'd hoped to catch a glimpse of her when he'd stopped at the diner. Just to see her set his heart racing. Could she be out with someone else? He quickly dismissed that disturbing thought. No, Maggie wouldn't allow herself to be with another man. He was certain of that after she'd told him about her painful past. He'd vowed to her that he'd never cause her any pain, and now he'd broken that vow. He'd broken her trust and he doubted he'd ever get it back. But damn it, he had to try!

He picked up the rose, got out of his truck, and walked to the trailer. He laid the rose on the top step. He stood for a few minutes in the bleak, lonely driveway staring at her home, remembering his happy times there, then climbed back into the truck and slowly backed down the driveway.

CHAPTER ELEVEN

Tom Morgan rushed over to Maggie. "My God, what's going on?" He threw his arms around her.

Maggie rested her tired head against his chest. She felt like a little girl seeking comfort from her father. Right now she wished she were a child seeking comfort in her mother's loving arms. Her mother had always made everything all right. This was the part of being an adult she hated. There was no parent to wipe her tears, chase away her fears, and make everything all right once again. She had to make her own pain go away and heal her hurts by herself. But having good friends did lighten the load, even if they couldn't change the world for her the way her mother used to.

"I'm sorry, Tom, I didn't know who else to call."

"No, no, you did the right thing," he quickly assured her. "I just can't believe Brant would arrest you. Are you all right?"

She nodded. "Just humiliated."

"I'll get you the best lawyer money can buy, Maggie. He

won't get away with this."

"No," she said firmly. "I didn't do anything, Tom." She rubbed her tired eyes. "I don't need a lawyer. The judge will believe me when I tell my side of the story."

He released her and then laid a fatherly hand on her shoulder. "Let me give you some advice, honey. There's no sense trying to fight Brant by yourself. Let me call Jason Lightman. He's the best."

Her eyes flashed. "No, don't you get it, Tom? If I do that, he'll win. I can't let him prevail especially since I didn't do anything wrong. I don't want to get off on a minor offense. That would look like I was guilty of something and I'm not. I'm innocent." Her words came out in a rush.

He slowly let his breath out. "Don't you understand, Maggie? He already has won in his sick mind." He shook his head, peering into her eyes. "Let go before he completely destroys you."

Her anger bubbled and then rose to the surface. "It's not right," she hoarsely whispered. "Tom, it's just not right." Tears of frustration stung her eyes.

"I know, Maggie, but no one can beat Brant. He's got too many on his payroll. He'll chew you up and spit you out into little pieces." He ran a weary hand over his face. "I can't stand to see you go through any more hurt. The sooner you put this behind you, the better."

"Someone's got to be able to do something! We can't keep letting him get away with this. How many more innocent lives is he going to be allowed to destroy? How many, Tom? He doesn't care. Destroying innocent people is a game with him. He's void of any real feelings or emotion."

"It's a sickness with him. He is a man without a conscience, and that's the worst kind of human being anyone can come up against."

"I don't know what I ever did to him, Tom. Why is he bent on destroying me?"

"With a man like Brant, sometimes your only fault is to have been born," he bitterly replied.

"Tom, you know I never threatened Janna's life, and she knows it too." Her voice cracked and then broke. "He couldn't wait to tell me that Chelsea Howard is expecting Chris's baby." Her eyes brimmed with tears. "How could Chris do this to me after all we've shared together?" she moaned. "I thought I meant something to him. I really did," she cried. "I loved him so much! Now he's made me feel so worthless. Why is my world falling apart?"

Tom gathered her into his arms and held her close to his chest again as he gently rubbed her back. "I know about the baby, honey. Chris came by the diner before closing and told me."

She pulled away from his embrace. "What? Why would he do that? What is wrong with everyone? Was he trying to rub salt in the wound?"

"No, Maggie," he said in a soothing voice. "He was trying to get me to plead his case with you." He searched her eyes. "I don't know what's going on with him, but he's a hurting man. Whatever mess he's gotten himself mixed up in is definitely not agreeing with him. I've never seen a man look so miserable."

"Brant's probably somehow behind that too."

"Maggie, I'm sorry that he's targeting you. No one will do anything to stop him. Everyone is afraid of him. How many have tried and failed?" He paced to the other side of the room and then back again. "Please let me call Jason. If you don't, I'm afraid you'll end up serving time in jail on trumped-up charges for something you never did." His voice shook. "Maggie, I don't know much about serving time, but I don't think you'd survive."

Her eyes clouded. "I've already done time, Tom. Have you forgotten?"

"It would be worse this time, Maggie. Brant would certainly see to it." He laid a hand on her shoulder. "Please let me make the call."

She wrung her hands. "To get out of this I'll have to plead guilty for something I never did. How fair is that?"

"It's not fair, but right now it's the only way." His brow furrowed. "At least let me give Jason a call so he can arrange bail and get you out of here tonight. Maybe he'll come up with a plan to beat Brant at his own game."

****

Janna seated herself on the sofa next to Chelsea. "This is such a cozy little place," she said.

Chelsea frowned. "It won't do for the three of us after the baby comes. Chris, would you fix Janna a drink?" she asked. When he didn't respond, her voice rose shrilly. "Chris!"

"What?" He looked questioningly at Chelsea. "I'm sorry, what did you say?"

"I asked you to fix Janna a drink," she replied exasperated. "Is something wrong, Chris? You've been distracted all evening."

He walked to the portable liquor cabinet. "I'm fine," he stiffly answered. "What would you like, Janna?"

"Some wine will be fine, Chris."

"What about you, Chelsea? Would you care for some wine also?"

She shot him a dirty look. "You know I can't drink while I'm pregnant. Alcohol can harm the baby."

He shrugged and then poured a glass of wine for Janna and a Scotch and water for himself. He carried the drinks over to the sofa and handed Janna her drink, then took his and seated himself in an easy chair. He tried to keep his mind focused on Janna and Chelsea's silly chattering, knowing Chelsea expected him to be hospitable to their guest, but their topics of conversation bored him to tears. With Maggie, he'd had intellectual conversations that consisted of world events as opposed to Janna and Chelsea's ridiculous musings over the latest lip-gloss or eyeliner. He took a swallow of his drink and smiled halfheartedly at them.

Janna smoothed a napkin over her lap. "How've you been feeling?" Her eyebrows furrowed. "Are you suffering much from morning sickness? I heard it can be horrible."

Chelsea tossed her pretty head. "Actually, no. I've been feeling wonderful, and the baby is healthy. I'm getting more excited every day wondering what he's going to look like and who he'll act like—me or Daddy." She grinned, shooting a look in Chris's direction.

He ignored her comments and averted her gaze by staring down into his drink.

"You're right, you will definitely need a bigger place once the baby comes," Janna observed, looking around the cramped apartment. "Have you looked at any houses yet? I can put you in touch with a wonderful real estate agent. She not only sells but leases homes as well."

"Not yet, but I have some places in mind. I'd love to see what the real estate agent might have available to rent for the time being. Eventually we hope to buy a house. I want it all...you know, white picket fence..." She giggled. "A huge backyard for our children—yes, I want at least four—to play in."

Chris almost choked on his Scotch.

"Since Chris is such a wonderful handyman, he can do a lot of the remodeling himself," she continued.

"With all you have to do, the baby will be here before you know it."

Chelsea smiled. "Yes, we have to get organized. I want to be married before the baby's birth too." She beamed. "I thought we'd have a small, intimate ceremony due to my condition, and of course you and Brant hopefully will stand up with us."

Janna squealed. "We'd love to. I know Brant will be as excited as I am. I'd love to help plan the wedding."

"Thank you. As soon as we decide on the date, I'll let you know."

Janna nodded enthusiastically. "You're absolutely glowing, Chelsea. I can't wait until Brant and I start a family."

Chris raised his eyebrows. *That's all this world needs is another Brant Evans*, he thought.

"Oh, that would be wonderful if you became pregnant, Janna. Our babies could grow up together," she gushed. "That would be so much fun!"

Chris yawned, then stretched. "Where's Brant tonight?" he asked, not really caring but wondering how long Janna would be staying.

"He's at the station. He arrested Maggie Allen this evening and he's finishing up the paperwork on her."

Chris's glass slipped from his hands, shattering as it hit the hardwood floor.

"Chris!" Chelsea snapped. "What's wrong with you?"

He bent down and with a shaking hand picked up the pieces of the glass. "I'm sorry, it slid out of my hand." His eyes met hers and he saw the fiery sparks. His heart thudded irregularly in his chest. He knew from Chelsea's cool gaze that she was miffed at his reaction to Maggie's predicament.

"What did Maggie do?" Chelsea asked, eager for the gossip Janna was dying to share.

Janna shot a glance in Chris's direction, then turned her attention back to Chelsea. "She made threats on my life."

Chelsea's eyes widened. "That's terrible! You must have been extremely frightened. I always suspected she was unstable."

"For God's sake, that's the most ridiculous thing I've ever heard," Chris scoffed. "Maggie wouldn't hurt a fly!"

"Of course you'd say that," Chelsea fumed. "Anything that concerns your precious Maggie Allen warrants your sympathies. Has it ever occurred to you that she may not be the sainted woman you seem to think she is? It's time to remove her from the pedestal and face the truth."

Chris's jaw twitched as a quick retort came to his lips, but he just as quickly silenced himself. It was senseless to waste his breath on them. They'd never know Maggie the way he did. And he certainly wasn't about to defend her to the likes of those two with their petty nonsense.

"What happened, Janna?" Chelsea asked.

Janna bit her bottom lip as she slowly shook her head back and forth. "It was terrifying. She was like a madwoman. She became furious when she found out about you and Chris. She even had the nerve to accuse Brant and me of masterminding a plan to bring you two together. Can you believe it?"

Chelsea laughed. "That's ludicrous. Chris and I got together of our own free wills." She looked at Chris. "He couldn't wait to get me into bed. I suppose Maggie was a failure there too…or maybe it's her age."

Her look dared him to speak. He rolled his eyes as he met Chelsea's but maintained his vow of silence.

Janna chuckled.

"Was she *really* violent?" Chelsea leaned closer to Janna. "What did she do to you?"

Chris kept his eyes glued on Janna, watching every facial expression of phony terror exhibit itself as she only too happily retold her fabricated story. If he hadn't despised her before, he did now.

"Let's just suffice it to say that I saw a side of Maggie Allen I'd never seen before. I was afraid she was going to physically harm me." She shuddered as her eyes flitted back and forth in her beautiful head, embellishing all the sympathy Chelsea held for her. "She told me that I'd be sorry. It was the look in her eyes that frightened me most of all. She was like a wild woman totally out of control. And to think she'd make that kind of a threat in a public establishment. It makes me wonder what she would have done if the encounter wasn't in a public place. I sincerely believe she would have murdered me."

Chelsea slowly let her breath out. "Brant must have been furious."

"He was livid, and I pleaded with him not to have any charges preferred against her. We wouldn't have, but Brant said she just wouldn't relent."

"What do you mean?"

"Brant went to the diner and tried to talk to her to get to the bottom of it. He was all set to forget this ugly incident, but she became confrontational to him and repeated the threat she'd made to me to him. She gave him no choice."

Chris abruptly stood up. "Please excuse me, Janna, but I have an early day tomorrow and I need to get some sleep."

Janna glanced at her diamond wristwatch. "I didn't realize it was so late. I really should be going."

"No, please stay awhile longer," Chelsea insisted, grabbing her hand.

"Stay as long as you'd like," Chris said walking to the small bedroom.

Once inside, he quietly closed the door. He could still hear their muffled voices through the paper-thin walls. He sat on the edge of the bed shaking his head back and forth. Now it made sense why Maggie's trailer had been dark. He didn't believe for a minute one word Janna had said. She didn't have it in her to hurt a fly. If Maggie had made any threats, then she must have been pushed over the edge not realizing what she was saying. But he doubted even that — he was certain she hadn't said anything that could be construed as a threat.

He needed to talk to Maggie. She deserved to know the truth. He had to find a way to convince her that it was she he truly loved, not Chelsea. As soon as he could free himself of this mess with Chelsea, he intended to sit her down and make her listen. He would give his child, if it were truly his, his name, but not Chelsea. He could not bring himself to marry her. When the time was right, he would tell Chelsea what he intended to do. As long as he took care of his responsibility by providing for her and the baby, his obligation to her would be fulfilled. He'd paid a high price for his mistake, and now it was time to undo some of that damage. There was no way, though, that he was convinced this baby was his. His gut instinct gnawed at him to get to the truth. He needed to be tested as soon as possible. When the test came in, then he could begin to put his life back into some kind of order.

CHAPTER TWELVE

Shelly Burgess stood staring out of the window at her children, Terry and Tommy, as they played on the front lawn. A smile formed on her lips. They were the only good things that had come from her marriage. She'd fallen fast and hopelessly in love with Tyson Burgess at the age of eighteen, and after only two months of knowing him, they eloped. Her ideological fantasies of wedded bliss were soon shattered though when she discovered the rigorous demands of marriage with two children born in rapid succession.

She and Tyson soon started arguing over their lack of money and Tyson's frequent absences from home in his non-working hours. Then one bright, sunny spring day he informed her quite abruptly that he wasn't happy and couldn't see himself tied down to her for the rest of his life. He picked up his lunch pail, gave her a quick peck on the cheek, and walked out the door. She never saw him again.

Shelly quickly found employment at Tom's Diner, and

with the help of Family Services, she secured a lawyer to seek child support, but Tyson Burgess seemed to have disappeared off the face of the earth. She saved every dime she could and eventually obtained her divorce and put a deposit down on a small house for her and her boys. Times were hard, but owning her own home gave her a sense of security.

Even though she wasn't unhappy with her life, at times she still longed for a companion and a father figure for her young sons. As much as she wanted to hate Tyson for deserting her, she couldn't. A part of her would always love him, but she would never forgive him for abandoning his sons. Abandoning her was one thing, but how could he abandon his own flesh and blood? She pitied him knowing that someday he would regret never having the loving bond with their children that she did. She often wondered if he ever thought about the boys or her. If he did, would he ever become curious enough about them to try to contact them? If he ever did show up some dark, cold night at her door, what would her reaction be?

When the realization had finally set in that Tyson wasn't ever coming back, she'd been crushed and cried for days. Then anger set in. She'd never trust him again, and she seriously doubted she'd ever trust another man. After all, look where trust had gotten Maggie.

She'd thought that Maggie and Chris had the perfect relationship, but when she witnessed the pain and humiliation in Maggie's eyes as the truth about Chris and Chelsea's relationship became public knowledge, she suffered right along with Maggie wishing there was some way she could lessen some of the hurt. But she knew this was a journey Maggie needed to take by herself as she had done with the assurance that those who loved and cared about her would always be near with love and support.

She let her breath out in a huff. As far as she was concerned, there didn't exist an honest man anywhere on this planet. Her faith and hopes in finding a loyal, trustworthy man diminished with each passing day. It still didn't ease the loneliness in her heart though. It would be nice to have a pair of strong arms around her on the cold winter nights or the nights when she sat up with one of the boys when illness struck. But if a man for her existed, he was making himself unknown, so she strove to give her sons the best she could.

****

Maggie stared attentively at Jason Lightman. He was an unpretentious, clean-cut man who got right to the point. As much as she had grown to distrust lawyers, there was something about Jason that was very likable and made one feel he could be trusted. He looked comfortable and relaxed in his own skin. He was good-looking, but not in a noticeable way. On first glance there was nothing exceptional about him, but as he talked, his otherwise unobtrusive looks became more pronounced with the soothing tone of his voice and boyish-looking expressions suddenly appearing on his face. He had a firm jaw and clear, light green eyes. His nose had a slight bump on it causing Maggie to wonder if he'd broken it at some point in his life, but the bump made it appear that it was the only nose that would suit him. His sandy brown hair looked as though the wind had just blown through it without looking messy. He had a wholesome, healthy, outdoorsy look to him.

"What happens now?" she quietly asked.

"You'll be released on your own recognizance. The paperwork is being processed as we speak. I requested release with no bail and it was agreed to without question." He smiled.

"I don't think the state has to worry about you disappearing, and the judge agreed." His eyes clouded. "If Janna Evans doesn't drop the charges, then a court date will be scheduled and we'll prepare for trial, unless you want to plead guilty."

"I didn't do anything," Maggie insisted. "It's not right. I shouldn't be going through this." She angrily swept her hair from her brow.

He frowned, eyeing her carefully. "I believe you, Maggie, but we'll have to convince a jury to also believe you if Janna insists upon pursuing these charges against you."

"Jason, you know what kind of man Brant Evans is," Tom said.

"Everybody does, but the law is the law. I don't like it any more than you do, Tom."

"It's a crock!" Tom's lips curled in disgust.

Maggie shook her head. "This whole thing is like a horrible nightmare. I never threatened Janna with bodily harm. I feel like I've already been convicted before I even go to trial."

"As I said, I believe you, but it's the jury you need to convince. Brant Evans will use anything he can to discount your innocence." He was thoughtful for a minute. "He seems to have a personal vendetta against you."

"That's obvious, but I don't know why. I've never done anything to him."

"Maybe something so innocent it slipped your mind?" he questioned.

"No...nothing."

"Well, he'll try to dig up anything he can from your past no matter how seemingly insignificant. So if anything should come to mind, let me know immediately."

Tom turned to Maggie. "You never met him until you

109

began working in the diner, did you?"

"No. It doesn't make any sense." She cocked an eye. "I have nothing to hide, so there is nothing he can bring up about me."

"Are you certain of that?"

Her eyes widened. "Of course! What could I possibly have to hide? My life has been an open book for the past few years. All I've tried to do was pick up the pieces of my life and begin fresh, and now these ridiculous charges have been levied against me." She threw her hands up in revulsion.

Jason gave her a sympathetic look. "I well understand how you feel. But in any event, if there is anything you're unaware of, Brant is sure to find it. If anything comes to mind that you think I should be made aware of, please don't hesitate to get in touch with me immediately." He patted her shoulder. "And try not to worry."

"I'm not worried, because I'm innocent." She rubbed her eyes. "It's still not right that innocent people can be placed under arrest and charged with a crime that was not committed."

"Just goes to show what kind of world this has come to," Tom answered.

****

"I thought you were going to bed," Chelsea said.

Chris slowly walked back and forth, deep in thought, hands rammed into his pockets. He abruptly stopped, then suddenly whirled on her. "I'm too worked up to sleep."

She rolled her eyes. "I suppose it has to do with Maggie," she sarcastically retorted.

His eyes narrowed. "What do you know about the charges Brant and Janna have against Maggie?"

She shrugged innocently, her lips drawing up into a pout.

110

"Nothing more than what Janna told us." Her eyes searched his. "It sounds like Maggie has quite a vindictive temper though."

"Why do you say that?" he sharply asked.

She frowned. "Well, she's obviously upset because you left her for me. Some women can't take rejection, and she didn't know what to do with all that pent-up fury so she took it out on Janna. The sad thing is that Janna was only trying to be a friend to her and Maggie turned on her." She pointed a manicured finger at Chris. "You should have been man enough to tell her about us yourself. Since you didn't, Janna wanted to go to her as a friend to soften the blow instead of Maggie hearing the news from a stranger."

Chris's jaw dropped. "I can't believe I heard you correctly." He inhaled deeply. "I can't get the point across to you without sounding malicious, but there seems to be no other way to get it through your thick skull. I don't love you, Chelsea. It should be obvious to you that I've never loved you and that my feelings are never going to change. What part of that don't you understand? I would still be with Maggie today if you weren't pregnant. You and I do not have a relationship, we never did, and never will."

Her eyes fluttered and her long, made-up eyelashes quickly blinked. "You can't mean that, Chris. You and me and our baby are going to be a family." She glared at him. "Besides, I seem to recall that it didn't take much effort on my part to get you into bed," she sniffed sanctimoniously. "If memory serves me right, you were a more than willing participant. So you can quit your pompous, self-righteous act with me."

Chris's nostrils flared. "I'll do my moral duty, but don't expect anything more. The baby will carry my name if it's mine, but I swore to God, and I'll keep my vow, that I'll never touch you again!" He stormed out of the room, then out of the apartment, and jumped into his truck.

****

Brant stripped his clothes off then walked to the bathroom. Through the steamy shower glass door, he made out Janna's enticing body. He grew hard as he slowly pushed the door open.

She turned and a seductive smile formed on her lips. She held her arms out. "Just in time to wash my back," she purred.

He sucked in his breath, watching as her eyes traveled down to his cock. "I have something else in mind."

He pulled her to him with such force that he saw the fear briefly appear in her eyes. His hunger and passion for her tonight was almost suffocating him. He was a wild animal out of control. Would she let loose for just once and love him with the wild abandon he craved? He'd make her. He'd bring her to the edge until she begged for more.

She moaned as he pinned her to the shower stall, his moist, hungry mouth seeking out hers. Her hands clutched his strong shoulders, her nails digging into his flesh. He groaned as his passion mounted and the steaming water from the showerhead beat down on his back.

****

Maggie slammed her fist on the kitchen table. She was dammed if she'd let Brant Evans destroy her. She'd done nothing to him or his wife. She wasn't quite sure how she would do it, but knew that she had to be strong and stand up to him. She'd be the one to take him down, and when she did, everyone he'd ever hurt would have their just desserts. He'd get what he had coming to him for a long time. All she could do now, though, was bide her time. She hated the anger

112

inside of her steaming and coming to a boil. It was against her very nature, but she had no control over it. Brant Evans had brought out the worst in her. She'd never considered herself a fighter, but now she'd been thrown into the ring and if she stood still and did nothing to defend herself, he would certainly win the round.

She studied the single rose she held in her hand. She'd found it lying on her doorstep when she returned. There was no note, just this beautiful, single red rose. She filled a vase with water and placed the rose in it. She set the vase on the kitchen table, then pulled up a chair and propped her face in her hands as she stared at the rose. A solitary tear slid from her eye. Chris used to leave single roses for her. Sometimes she'd find a single red rose on her pillow as she slipped into bed at night or on the table in a vase when she returned from work. It was always one single red rose. She knew it was from Chris, and she knew by displaying it that she was opening her heart for more grief. Why did love have to hurt so much? Why couldn't she erase him from her mind as easily as she had let him into her heart? When would the pain finally stop and her heart stop jumping at the sound of his name? She prayed for the day that the mention of his name would evoke no emotional response.

****

Chris sat drumming his fingers on the steering wheel. He longingly watched Maggie's silhouette through the curtains, and his heart pounded sending the blood rushing to his head. He wanted her so desperately; he'd never wanted another woman or needed a woman as much as he did her. How did she react when she found the rose? Did she know it was from him? Surely, she knew. Would she proudly display it or toss

113

it in the trash? He couldn't blame her if she tore every petal from it.

He ran a hand over his unshaven chin feeling the rough stubble. "I'll win you back," he vowed. "I'll find a way to win you back." He saw the lights go out and the trailer was swallowed up in the starless night. His heart felt as black as the night. He was empty without her. There was no meaning to his life anymore. He kept his eyes riveted on the darkened trailer for a few minutes, yearning to be inside with her, to be snuggled up in bed next to her where he should be. He shivered as he started the engine and with headlights off slowly backed away.

Twenty minutes later, he peeled off his clothes and slipped into bed. He felt Chelsea's arms encircle him. He stiffened as he turned his back to her.

"We need to talk, Chris," she quietly said. She turned the bedside lamp on. "I don't want to argue. It's not good for the baby. I just want to talk like two civilized adults."

He let his breath out in a rush. "We have nothing to talk about. I've got a long day tomorrow and need to get some sleep."

"Yes, we do have things to talk about," she insisted. "I want to be married before the baby is born. Once we're married and the baby comes, I know things will be different between us, Chris. Our relationship got off on the wrong foot, that's all."

He turned on his side to face her, propping himself up on one arm. "Chelsea, why do you want to marry me? My God, I know you don't really love me, and I've made it clear that I'm not in love with you and never have been. How many times do I have to say it before you'll believe it? What is it going to take for you to understand?"

Her eyes flickered. "I want the baby to come into this world with his parents married and sharing the same name, not just a bed."

Chris grunted. "We don't share a bed in the sense that most couples do. What happened between us never should have. Marriage for the sake of the baby would be a big mistake. The kid would grow up sensing the tension and lack of affection between you and me. It wouldn't be fair to any child to be brought into the world under those circumstances." He sighed heavily. "I'll provide well for you and the baby, you know that. But that's all I'll do."

She lowered her eyes. "I want us to get married as soon as possible, Chris. We need to think about looking for a bigger place soon too. The baby will be here before we know it, and we've done nothing to prepare."

"You apparently haven't been listening to a word I've been saying, have you?" He leaned nearer toward her. "I've been doing a lot of thinking lately, Chelsea. How do I know for certain that the baby is really mine?" He closely watched her reaction. "I'd be a fool to claim your child as mine until I had positive proof."

She cringed as her bottom lip began to tremble. "How can you ask such a horrible question?" she cried. "That's an appalling thing to say."

"I'm looking out for my own ass," he stated. "It's about time I did."

She sniffed. "You've changed, Chris. What happened to that sweet, kind man I once knew?"

He laughed mockingly. "He got tricked by you and had his whole world turned upside down."

Chelsea peered into his eyes. "You can't get Maggie Allen

out of your mind, can you? No woman will ever be able to take Maggie's place in your heart."

He ignored her question. "I want to be tested. I want proof that the baby you're carrying is really mine and not someone else's."

Her eyes widened brimming with tears ready to spill. "The baby is yours, Chris. I can't believe you would ever doubt it."

"If the test proves the baby is indeed mine, then I'll take care of you. But I refuse to make any kind of plans or to move into a bigger apartment with you until I know for certain. And even if the baby is mine, I don't intend to spend the rest of my life with you, Chelsea."

Tears spilled from her eyes. "I can't believe what I'm hearing, Chris," she sniffed. "But if that's what it takes then fine, I'll make the arrangements."

He warily eyed her. "I'll make the necessary arrangements myself."

"You don't trust me?" she asked in a wobbly voice.

"Give me a break, Chelsea. You've never given me cause to trust you."

"We could try to work things out." She twisted a strand of her hair between her thumb and index finger. "If we worked together, we could make a life together. I know we could, Chris. Why can't you even give us a chance?"

He loudly exhaled. "There's nothing to work out. Even if the baby is mine, it will not change the fact that I don't love you and don't want to spend my life with you. Tomorrow I'll call my doctor and make arrangements for the test."

"If that's what it'll take for you to accept the fact that this child is yours." Her eyes lowered to her stomach.

"That's what it will take." He rolled over onto his back and then turned to his side, his back facing her.

CHAPTER THIRTEEN

Maggie worked the counter, making idle conversation with the two truck drivers who were perched on stools in front of her as they gulped their breakfasts before heading out for a long day on the road. They were nice guys who arrived every morning, rain or shine, and she enjoyed their morning chitchat, which was usually filled with trivia. She was relieved they hadn't mentioned her arrest, in fact, none of her customers had all morning, but she was certain they wondered. Her arrest and the details of it were prominently displayed in this morning's paper.

Tom wanted her to take some time off until things blew over and had even offered to pay her, but she'd held firm to her convictions, determined to hold her head high and show everyone that she had nothing to hide. Those who knew her and cared about her didn't doubt her innocence, of that she was certain. She needed to get back to some semblance of a normal life, and the only way she could do that was to go on about her normal, daily routine.

Shelly touched her arm. "Maggie, I'm sorry about last night," she whispered. "You should have called me."

"Thanks, Shell, but I knew you had plans with Terry and Tommy. I would never be able to forgive myself if they had to miss the opening of the newest action movie," she replied with a wink. "How'd it go?"

Shelly laughed. "We had a blast. Of course, when we got home they had to reenact the whole movie. I wish I could keep them at this age forever."

Maggie nodded. "I've heard it said that these are going to be some of the best years of your life. It must be a beautifully indescribable feeling knowing that you've brought them into the world and you'll always be a part of one another no matter what," she wistfully stated.

Shelly's eyes misted. "I'm sorry about Chris and Chelsea. It must have been a shock. I still can't believe it." Her eyes suddenly narrowed. "Something's not right. It doesn't make any sense. Chris isn't that kind of man, at least not the Chris Jacoby I always knew."

Maggie composed herself. "Unfortunately, people change, and I guess it hurts more when it is someone we don't expect it from. It just goes to show that we don't always know someone as well as we think we do." She looked into Shelly's troubled eyes. "I'll be okay. It wasn't meant to be for Chris and me. No matter how much I wanted it and yearned for it, it wasn't in the cards." She took a deep breath. "Besides, its friends like you who make life worthwhile." She flashed Shelly a bright smile.

"Let's get together this weekend. I promised the boys I'd take them to the zoo." Her eyes sparkled. "Come on with us, it'll be fun. They're always asking me why you haven't been around for so long. They'd love to see you!"

She grinned. "It has been ages since I've seen them. I can't think of anyone I'd rather spend my weekend with." She squeezed Shelly's shoulder. "Thanks."

Shelly suddenly tensed. "Just what you need right now," she groaned as her eyes drifted to the entrance of the diner.

"What's the matter?" Maggie asked as she followed Shelly's gaze. Her breath momentarily caught in her throat. "What does he want?" she asked watching Chris making his way toward her.

"Hi, Maggie...Shelly."

Shelly nodded a greeting.

"Maggie, can I talk to you for a minute?" he quietly asked.

She met his eyes and then looked away. Her brief glance showed how tired he looked with sagging dark circles underneath his normally sparkling eyes. "There's nothing to talk about, Chris."

"Please, Maggie," he begged. "I'll only take a few minutes of your time. You need to hear me out. Just this one time. I promise if you do then I won't bother you ever again if that's what you want."

"I'll cover for you, Maggie," Shelly offered. "Why don't you take your break?"

"No, Shelly. Thanks anyway." She looked at Chris, straightening her shoulders. "There is nothing to discuss, Chris. What's done is done. You need to go home and take care of Chelsea."

"No, Maggie. Please listen to what I have to say."

She shook her head. "Chelsea needs you, Chris, especially now that she's expecting your baby."

"Maggie, I don't think the baby's mine," he whispered.

119

"I'm going to be tested."

She frowned as she looked into his eyes once again. His eyes were now filled with hope. "Whether the test proves you are or aren't the biological father of Chelsea's baby, Chris, doesn't excuse the fact that you slept with her. You hurt me, Chris." She blinked. "I didn't deserve that, not from you. I'm finally getting my life straightened out and back on track. Please just stay out of my life and let me go on with mine."

He shifted his weight from one foot then to the other. "I made a horrible mistake, and my life is hell without you." He stared into her eyes. "Are you really getting on with your life, Maggie?" His voice was tender. "You shouldn't have been arrested. I want to help you through this."

"I agree that I shouldn't have been arrested, but it doesn't change the fact that this morning's paper is filled with it. But I intend to stand by my innocence."

"Anyone who knows you, Maggie, knows you're innocent. Let me help you through it, Maggie. I'm not asking for anything more than your friendship. All I care about is helping you."

"If you are sincere and really want to help me, Chris, then please just stay away from me."

****

Janna set her hairbrush down and turned with a start when Brant entered the bedroom. "Hi, honey." She blushed. "You were in such a strange mood last night." Her face reddened even more than it was. "Of course I'm not complaining…it was just so unexpected. It was wonderful and so different for us." She touched his hand. "I didn't want to break the spell by asking you all sorts of questions about your meeting with Nick Saunders. I take it from your mood last night that all went well."

His jaw twitched, but it was the strange look in his eyes that worried her. "I just needed to hold on to you. I hope I didn't frighten you or harm you in any way last night."

"No, Brant it was an experience I never expected." Her eyes sparkled with the remembrance. Afterward, they hadn't spoken but went to bed and made love again before falling asleep wrapped in one another's arms. "Honey, what's the matter? Did I do something wrong?"

"No, you were perfect," he quickly assured her, then turned and looked toward the window. "It's the strangest thing, Janna." He walked to the window. "You'll never believe it. I'm still reeling from the shock of it." He placed his hands on the windowsill.

"Just tell me, baby. I want us to share everything."

He turned around and looked at her. He thoughtfully rubbed his temples. "I inherited over twenty million dollars."

"Brant! Twenty million dollars? That's wonderful news!" Janna exclaimed.

"There's more. Along with the inheritance, I found out I also have a sister." His mouth twisted into an ugly smirk.

"A sister? Did Nick give you the details?" She grabbed his hands. "Tell me about your sister, Brant. I know you must have so much going through your mind right now. No wonder you didn't want to talk about it last night."

He snorted. "That's putting it mildly. My life is a mess!"

"Honey, how can you say that? You've just inherited twenty million dollars and found out you have a sibling."

"That's not the point, Janna," he bitterly replied. "I have a sister and the bitch got as much money as I did."

"Why are you being so harsh with someone you don't even know? She may be as shocked as you are to find out she has a brother. Why don't you arrange to meet her face to face? Maybe it will make you feel better actually seeing her as a flesh and blood person. She may be experiencing some of the same emotions as you."

His eyes smoldered. "It's not as simple as that." He intently fixed his gaze on her. "Imagine for just a moment, if you will, that the person you most despise in this world turns out to be your blood relative…how ironic is that?"

His remark was more of a statement than a question, and Janna took her time trying to absorb his feelings and emotions. "You already know her, Brant? Is that what has you so upset?"

His jaw twitched involuntarily, and a faraway look appeared in his eyes. "Yes, I know her. You do too."

She was almost afraid to ask her next question but knew she had to. The tension that hung in the air wouldn't be dissipated until she knew. "Who is she?" She watched his facial expressions.

His complexion drained of color and he looked sick like he would vomit at any moment. "Maggie Allen," he finally spat out. "Maggie Allen is my sister."

Her eyes widened in shock as her brow shot up. She couldn't have heard him correctly. She had to be mistaken. "Did you say Maggie Allen?" she whispered.

He stuffed his hands into his pockets. "Can you believe it? Of all the women on this planet, Maggie Allen has to be the one."

"My God, Brant. It doesn't make any sense. How can Maggie possibly be your sister? There has to be a mistake."

"Oh, if you knew my father, it makes perfect sense." He laughed bitterly. "It just puts so much into perspective now."

"Does Maggie know?"

"I don't think so. If she had known, then I doubt she would

122

have kept it private. It would be just like her to rub it in."

"Why would she rub it in, Brant? It isn't her fault what your father and her mother did. She is no more to blame than you are." She shrugged. "Well, it looks like her financial troubles are over. That should help to soften the blow of this news."

Brant's eyes blazed. "If I had my way, she wouldn't see a dime of that money."

"Honey, you can't prevent her from collecting her share of the inheritance. After all, your father left it to her. Whether you like it or not, he wanted her to have it."

He scowled. "I know that, but believe me, if there were a way to keep her from getting her hands on any of it, I'd do it." He shook with rage.

His anger frightened her. His pasty complexion suddenly changed to a blazing red. He looked like an overripe tomato ready to explode at any moment. She'd never seen him this enraged before. "Try to calm down, Brant. I know it must have been a blow to find out that Maggie Allen of all people is your sister. I wish I had been there with you when you received the news."

"It wouldn't have changed the outcome whether you were with me or not!" He wildly threw his hands in the air.

"I'm sure it's worse because you never had a clue." She was thoughtful for a minute. "Or did you? Did you know Maggie's mother?"

"No. I never met her, at least not that I can remember."

"I don't know what to say, honey. I wish I could help."

He paced across the carpet. "I just can't believe that my father had so much compassion for Maggie's mother. I never knew he was capable of such strong emotions." He frowned.

"Why did he stay with my mother all these years if he didn't love her? Why couldn't he even one time act like he cared about her?"

"Brant, some of your questions may always remain unanswered. In his own way, I'm sure he cared about what happened to your mother. Do you think your mother had an inkling of this indiscretion?"

"I really doubt it. I'm sure if she had known, I would have gotten wind of it. Maggie's parentage certainly would have been mentioned at some point. When my parents argued, as they frequently did, all the dirty laundry was aired repeatedly. I began to know by heart what they were going to say when the battle began. No, my mother would have never kept this to herself. I'm certain of it."

"If your father managed to keep your mother in the dark all these years, then it proves how far he went to keep this part of his life a secret. Do you suppose that's why he put such a strict age restriction on the inheritance?"

"It's the only logical explanation I can come up with. I suppose he assumed I'd be able to handle the news better at thirty instead of twenty."

"But you aren't able to, are you, Brant?"

He stopped pacing and stood in front of her. "I don't think it would have mattered if he'd put the age restriction at fifty. I would still feel the same." He ran his hand through his hair. "I feel so damned betrayed. He's made a fool not only of my mother but of me." He fumed as he resumed his pacing. "I suppose, though, if there is any comfort in this whole mess, it's that my mother isn't alive to have to bear it. She would have never been able to face this shame and humiliation."

"I wonder if your father was ever in contact with Maggie. Do you think he discreetly placed himself in her life when major events were occurring for her even without her knowledge?"

"I don't think so, but at this point anything's possible. According to Nick, Maggie's mother refused any contact with my father. The man Maggie assumed was her biological father raised her as his own, and it's doubtful that he even knew that Maggie wasn't his." He sighed. "Nick says my father wrote a personal letter to Maggie and he will be taking it, along with her check, to her tomorrow."

"He's going to deliver it in person? Why?"

"That's the type of guy Nick is. Remember, he and my father go back a long way and his loyalty to my father is at times almost obscene."

"It could be that the man who raised Maggie knew he wasn't her biological father. Have you thought about that possibility?"

He frowned. "If he did, he took it to the grave with him. All we have are suppositions. But then we don't know what went on in Maggie's home as she was growing up either. All we know is how motivated she was to make her mark in the corporate world." He squinted. "Where did that motivation come from?"

Janna's brow furrowed. "This news is bound to devastate Maggie. She's been through so much lately."

"I suppose it will." He shot her a suspicious look. "But I don't really care how the bitch feels."

"Honey, when you found out this news, was that the reason you insisted I file charges against Maggie? Was it a revenge thing, Brant?"

He kept silent.

She grabbed his arm. He stopped pacing across the carpet. "Honey, this vendetta against Maggie has to stop. It's not healthy."

"What vendetta?" he demanded.

"Come on, Brant. This is me you're talking to…your wife! Ever since I've known you, you've had this rage festering inside of you whenever you hear the name Maggie Allen. What's going on?"

He sat on the edge of the bed. A dark cloud moved over his face. "All of my life I've felt overshadowed by that bitch. It never made sense to me then why my father followed her career like a hawk taking every opportunity to rub it in my face about her successes. He was like a man obsessed at times." His voice was angry. "It didn't matter what I ever accomplished. No, nothing I did was ever good enough for him."

Janna massaged his shoulders as he talked. His voice was self-pitying, almost childlike as he spoke. She felt his pain. He'd been competing throughout his childhood, but never knew whom he was competing against. His own insecurities and weaknesses forced him to strive for power.

"He saved every magazine and newspaper clipping that even remotely mentioned her." He stiffened. "I grew to hate her just by her name and endeavors. I never met her, but she'd become a thorn in my side. That's why I began to follow her life and career. I was looking for a clue — anything that would explain my father's strange fascination with her." He sighed heavily. "Nick's news filled in all of the missing pieces. I should have sensed it and questioned it. My mother should have. He flaunted his bastard right in front of us and we never suspected a thing. How could we have been so damned naïve? My father kept Maggie nearby, following her life even though he couldn't physically be a part of it. I suppose it was the only way he could keep his firstborn close to him."

Janna listened intently but didn't speak. Brant needed to

unburden himself and release all the bitterness he'd harbored most of his life. The best thing she could do for him was to just sit and listen without giving her own observations, even though she had plenty. His anger and hatred had festered all these years and now was ready to erupt, spewing the filth from the core of his being upon anyone who crossed his path. She understood him now, and now that she did, it frightened her even more.

His lips drew tight together. "No matter what I did, it was never good enough. He took every opportunity to let me know about her corporate advances." He laughed bitterly. "I could never figure out why her life mattered so much to him. I assumed he was trying to make a point because not only was she a woman, she also came from a middle class family and had still managed to make a prominent mark on society. Her accomplishments, I suppose, were to motivate me into being a high achiever. It was as though he wanted me to become so angry that I'd go out and achieve even more than she had." He let his breath out in a rush. "It's hell."

Janna sat next to him and slipped her arm through his. "It must have been a difficult time for you, Brant," she softly said.

"Yes, more than anyone could ever imagine, but now it all makes perfect sense." His jaw tightened. "He was more enamored with his whore's little bastard than he was of his legitimate child. She was the child he cared about, the child he wished he'd been raising. I was like a second-class citizen to him. He didn't love my mother so how was he expected to love me? I think I was a mistake and he only stayed with my mother to make himself look good. Appearances were important to him so he certainly had to keep his up!" he sneered.

She drew him into her arms. "It'll be all right, honey. The

127

truth is out now. I'm here, and we'll get through this together. You need to talk about all of these emotions."

"No, she needs to pay for what she's done to me!" he cynically retorted.

"Who? Maggie's mother? She died years ago, honey."

"No, Maggie!"

"But Maggie didn't personally do anything to you, Brant. She's not to blame for any of this."

"She was born. That's enough for me!"

CHAPTER FOURTEEN

Tom finished his paperwork, closed the account book, and placed it in the desk drawer. He stood up and stretched, then walked out of his office closing the door behind himself. He made his way to the back of the counter, grabbed a cup from underneath, and poured himself some coffee. He picked up his cup of coffee and the afternoon's paper, walked to a secluded booth, and settled into it. He set his coffee down and spread the newspaper out.

He enjoyed this time of the day. In a little over an hour, the diner would be closing for the day. A few stragglers would come in for a quick cup of coffee or piece of pie. The regulars all knew the hours, and Tom's busiest times of the day were the early morning breakfast rush and lunchtime crowd. After three o'clock, business slowed. He always closed at promptly six o'clock every night and opened at five thirty every morning. The hours were long and hard, but he wouldn't have it any other way. This was the only life he knew and the only life he cared to know. He was fortunate that he'd been able to make his dream come to fruition, and he prided himself on his diner.

After his stint in the Army, he'd come back to Cedar Pines to realize his vision. He'd never been a man of extravagance or one to set his sights on lofty goals. All he aimed for was a small eating establishment that would provide him enough of an income to afford a comfortable lifestyle with hopefully a wife and children someday. Maybe to some his dream wouldn't have seemed like much, but to him it was everything he'd ever wanted, and that's all that mattered. He was satisfied.

He knew he could have opened a fancy restaurant in an upscale section of the city, but he chose to settle in a less advantageous sector. This part of the city was where the real people lived. These men and women were the true backbone of society. They lived simple, unpretentious lives, not caring about the phony encumbrances of society. They worked long, hard hours for every dime they earned. They were the common people, and in Tom's opinion, the people he wanted to be a part of. These were his people.

He scanned the obituaries. It was the section of the newspaper he turned to first. He'd started his morbid ritual shortly after his heart attack. His health had suddenly made him think about his own mortality. So many of his friends had already passed from this world. Life was too short, and he wished he could turn back the clock and relive some of his most cherished days. How unfortunate that one never gained knowledge until later in life when as a youth it would have been so much more useful. But then that was the irony of life.

In his younger days, he thirsted to see and experience everything this world had to offer, knowing that he had all the time in the world at his disposal. It seemed in youth that time would go on forever, but as each year passed, he was jolted to the reality of how quickly the days now seemed to come together. Things that had been put off for another day rapidly piled up now and probably would never get accomplished. Not in one lifetime. Love was a lot like that too, he mused. Some men spent their entire lives going from one woman to another, never seeming to find the one to build lasting memories with. But he'd been contented with only one.

His thoughts wandered to Milly. Not a day went by that he didn't think about her. God, how he missed her. He'd felt so cheated when she was suddenly snatched from him. He'd never even had the remotest interest in another woman since her, and he knew he never would. Milly was one of a kind and to him she would remain as close to a goddess as a woman could get. She was irreplaceable, and his only comfort came from the fact that he knew someday he would be rejoined with her. On his low days that thought was the only thing that seemed to keep him going.

Milly was a beauty with classic good looks and breeding. She had set her sights on him in their senior year of high school. He was the captain of the football team, and she was head cheerleader. He was on the shy side and never used the jock status to his advantage. He was a simple person and lived a simple life following the golden rule as his parents and grandparents had taught him of doing unto others.

He knew that what you gave out you eventually got back, even if at times it didn't seem true. He believed that everyone had something worthwhile to contribute to society no matter how small. His tastes were straightforward, and when Milly started showing an interest in him, at first he didn't know what she expected. There were many boys interested in her, certainly many better-looking and with money to spend. He'd hear them talk about her in the locker room, but she never gave any of them the time of day. He wondered why she'd been so attracted to him, when he didn't have much to offer and probably never would.

He was greatly relieved when he soon learned that her values and morals were the same as his. She was the sweetest, gentlest woman he'd ever met. Not once had he ever heard an unkind word toward another pass her lips. It wasn't hard for her to steal his heart, and he knew she kept it safely beating next to her own. When he completed his service to the Army, he came home and asked Milly to be his wife. He explained to her his excitement about someday opening a small diner. She shared his dream and one starry summer night, they eloped, then came back and settled into a happily married blissful life. He took a job on the loading docks of a sawmill, and Milly found employment in a fabric mill. They put every dime they could spare, after their living expenses, into their savings account for the diner.

Five years later, they found the perfect place at a price they could afford. A year later, they both quit their jobs and jumped headfirst into the status of business owners. At Milly's insistence, they christened the diner "Tom's". Milly spent endless hours redoing the inside and making the diner into the homey, friendly place it still was. Tom experimented with recipes, finally excelling in several simple home-cooked varieties for his growing clientele. Everything would be cooked from scratch with Milly making all of the pies, breads, pastries, and rolls herself. They cheerfully and contentedly worked side-by-side, never minding the long hours but enjoying the business they'd created.

If there was a downside to their marriage, it was that they would never be blessed with a child of their own. After months of tests to determine why Milly couldn't get pregnant, it was learned that due to a serious childhood illness, Tom had been rendered sterile. The children they'd always talked about and dreamed of weren't going to happen. They discussed adoption, but never did much more than discuss it. Too many years had silently slipped by, and one day they realized it was too late. The demands of the restaurant occupied most of their free time, and they reassured one another in the end that it was probably for the best. They were happy and in love and felt fortunate just to be with one another. But at times Tom felt the loss and knew that Milly did also.

He wasn't prepared for the news Milly would share with him one crisp autumn day, shortly after their twentieth wedding anniversary. She'd returned in tears from a routine visit with her doctor. Tom knew she had been rundown and tired, but he attributed it to the demands of the expanding diner. She quietly sat him down and in the gentlest tone of voice she could muster told him that the doctor feared cancer but wouldn't know until more tests were run. The next few days were like a nightmare, but the worst was yet to come when the tests confirmed that Milly's beautiful body was riddled with cancer. His beloved Milly was going to die and there was nothing he could do about it. He tried to stay strong for her, but most of the time it was her optimism and strength that kept them both going. She refused to give up the fight, determined to live each day to the fullest.

She continued to work in the restaurant until she was too sick and weak to stand on her feet any longer. Tom hired a nurse to sit with her, and he took over the entire responsibilities of the restaurant. One of the saddest days was when he had to inform his loyal customers that Milly was no longer able to do the baking. He had to resort to ordering those items from a local bakery now, but he did what he had to do. His customers stayed with him, sorely missing Milly's presence in the diner. They'd become like family, rejoiced with him on Milly's good days, and cried with him on her bad days.

Before the New Year arrived, Milly was gone. One cold, stormy night, she peacefully died in their bed enclosed in his arms. He lay there and knew she was gone but refused to let her go. He needed to hold her for just awhile longer. He was thankful for her decision to spend her final days in her own bed instead of in a hospital.

Only at her death did he mourn the fact that they had never been able to have children. It would have eased his heart to have a part of her still here with him. All he had now were his memories. He felt her presence in every part of the apartment, and when he'd go downstairs to the diner, it was as though she'd never left. At times, he was certain he smelled her fresh, gentle scent of lilac. He'd look around expecting to see her but knew she wouldn't really be there. At times, his loneliness for her was almost unbearable. He was lost without Milly and knew that he would always be missing a part of himself until the day came when he would rejoin her.

Shelly and Maggie had both come into his life at the times he was feeling his lowest. Now they helped to fill the empty void by becoming the daughters he'd never had. When he had his sudden heart attack, they took turns nursing him back to health while keeping the diner running. Many mornings he'd awaken to find Maggie camped out on the sofa keeping a watchful eye on him. He wished he was able to offer them more income, but they didn't seem to mind. They were his family in every sense of the word, and every day he thanked God for sending them to him, but suspected that his angel

Milly may have had something to do with it. God, how he missed her.

"More coffee, Tom?" Shelly asked. "You look lost in thought."

Startled, he looked up at her. "Oh, no thanks, honey. I'll be heading upstairs in a few minutes."

Maggie slid in the booth next to him. "Everything's wiped down in the kitchen. It's been slow today." She yawned and then leisurely stretched. "Big plans tonight, Tom?"

He laughed. "Oh yeah! I've got a heavy date with my pillow and bed."

Maggie smiled studying his drawn face. "You look tired, Tom. Are you feeling all right?"

He patted her hand. "I'm fine, Maggie. Nothing that a good night's sleep won't cure."

"Are you sure?" she worriedly asked.

"Don't worry," he replied with a smile. "It's been a long week."

"I know," she said and sighed. "But please don't get stressed out over my situation."

His eyebrows shot up. "I'm not just going to sit by and watch you suffer alone."

"What would Shell and I ever do without you, Tom?"

"You know the feeling is mutual." He folded his newspaper.

"I wish I had known her," Maggie said quietly.

"Who?"

"Milly. That's who you were thinking about, wasn't it?"

He nodded. "I miss her so much, Maggie." His eyes glistened. "She would have loved you and Shelly."

"You were a wonderful husband to her, Tom."

135

"I hope I was. She was one of a kind. I never dreamed I would have been blessed to meet someone who was so much like me and shared all of the same dreams." He rubbed his eyes. "Look at me going on like this."

Shelly patted his shoulder. "Tom, if I found a man half as good as you, I'd be a happy woman."

Maggie nodded in agreement.

"You two are something else," he said with a hint of embarrassment in his voice.

"We mean it," Shelly assured him, "and don't you ever forget it. I think I'll check the sugar containers. Do you want a cup of coffee, Mag?"

She grinned. "No, I'm about all coffee'd out."

"Okay, then. Just yell if you change your mind." She grinned. "It doesn't mean I'll get it for you, but at least I'll know you want a cup."

Maggie and Tom laughed as Shelly sauntered away.

The tinkling of the bell on the door caused them all to look in that direction. They watched in silence as the well-dressed man made his way to the counter and spoke in an inaudible voice to Shelly. She motioned in their direction, and the man looked their way then slowly walked over to where they sat.

"Maggie Allen?" he asked extending a hand. "I'm Nicholas Saunders. It's nice to meet you. I'm an attorney for the Evans' family."

"How may I help you?" Maggie stiffly asked.

Tom held up a hand. "Wait a minute. If this is about the charges Janna Evans has filed against Maggie, she's being represented by Jason Lightman, and I don't think it would be wise for her to discuss anything without him being present."

A surprised look appeared on his face. "No...no," he quickly assured Tom. "This is an entirely different matter."

He pulled an envelope from his pocket and turned his attention to Maggie. "I suggest you take your time to absorb this information. My card is inside if there is anything you'd like to discuss. I'll be happy to answer any questions that I can." He handed her the envelope.

"I don't understand," she said her eyes sweeping over him.

He gestured to the envelope. "You will. Nice meeting you."

Maggie quizzically looked at Tom as Nicholas Saunders moved away from the booth. She looked down at the envelope she tightly held in her hand, then slowly opened it. She peered inside, then gradually pulled out the contents.

"Oh my God!" she shrieked.

CHAPTER FIFTEEN

"Chelsea, you seem so distracted. What's the matter?" Janna worriedly asked. "Is everything okay with the baby?"

"The baby's the only thing that's going right. Everything else in my life is a mess," she wined. "Nothing's going the way it's supposed to. I feel at loose ends not knowing which way to turn."

Janna sympathetically patted her shoulder. "Oh, sweetie, that's probably just your hormones making you feel that way." She smiled reassuringly. "Look at all the wonderful things about to happen in your life."

"Like what?" she complained. "My life is all screwed up!" She wrung her hands in despair. "I don't know what to do anymore, Janna."

"Come on! You're going to have a baby! You're going to be moving into a new home soon with Chris. You're going to be a married woman. All of those are wonderful, positive things happening for you."

"Getting Chris to marry me is like pulling teeth. He's fighting me at every turn." Her face puckered. "He doesn't want me. I'm scared and all alone."

"He's probably just got cold feet. Don't forget, it's a big step for him too. He's been single all these years and now he's going to have a wife and a baby. He needs time to adjust to everything. Everything has happened so suddenly that he's probably just overwhelmed."

She tossed her head. "No, he doesn't want a life with me and the baby. He said so himself. What he has is Maggie Allen in his blood, and he'll never stop loving her." She loudly exhaled. "You witnessed how he defends her at every turn. She can never do any wrong. I'd like to knock her off that damned pedestal he has her on," she bitterly replied.

She shrugged her shoulders. "Well, you do have to admit, Chelsea, that everything has happened like a whirlwind. He needs time to let everything soak in, and I'm sure he'll come around once it does. He's an honest, decent man and I know he'll do the right thing by you and the baby."

"He doesn't love me, Janna."

She thoughtfully tapped her fingernail on the coffee table. "Do you love him? Be honest, Chelsea. How do you feel about him?"

"That's not the issue."

"Isn't it? Come on, Chelsea. Marriage isn't something you should take lightly. It's going to be the most important commitment you're ever going to make." Her eyes glistened. "When you repeat those vows, those will be the most important words you'll ever speak." She grabbed Chelsea's hands. "Don't take those vows if you don't mean them."

Chelsea looked at her uncomfortably. "Are you that

139

deeply in love with Brant? So much that you could never envision yourself ever with anyone else?"

Her eyes glowed. "God, yes! I can't even explain how he makes me feel, Chelsea. I love him more than I ever thought it possible to love another human being. When I repeated those vows to him as I gazed into his eyes, I knew that his eyes were the eyes I wanted to see before I went to sleep every night and when I woke up every morning." She blushed. "Okay, I know I sound silly, but that's how Brant makes me feel. I don't know how I could even begin to live life without him. He's my world."

Chelsea smiled weakly. "I always believed that kind of love only existed in fairy tales or the imagination of some romance novelist."

Janna emphatically shook her head back and forth. "No, believe me. It exists in your heart when you find that one special person who takes your breath away and becomes so much a part of you that you don't know where you begin and he ends. You'll know it when it's real."

Chelsea ran a shaky hand through her hair. "Chris will never feel that way about me. I would be a fool to think he ever would."

"Do you feel that way about him? Maybe that's what this is really all about. Be true to yourself. If you don't, then you'll live to regret it. Don't take those vows unless you're certain that Chris is the man you want to spend the rest of your life with. Love him that deeply or let him go."

"But I'm carrying his child. It's too late."

"No, it's not, Chelsea. You can raise the baby alone. This isn't the fifties. It's acceptable today to have a child and raise it on your own. Women are choosing that option every day."

She anxiously threw her hands in the air. "But those

women planned to have their child alone. I'm not one of those types of women who can raise a child alone, Janna. I want my child to be raised with two parents."

"How fair is it for any child to be raised by two people who only harbor ill will for one another? How will that affect the child's own self-esteem and dignity? You need to carefully think it through, Chelsea. You need to do what's good not only for yourself, but most importantly for the baby."

"Janna, why are you saying these things to me? Whose side are you on? You sound like you want Maggie and Chris to get back together."

"That's not it at all, Chelsea. You're my best friend and I want you to be as happy when you marry as I still am today."

"In time I'm sure Chris and I will grow to love one another. Back through history marriages were prearranged and in many cases the couples barely knew one another or not at all. The first time many of them even laid eyes on one another was when they met at the ceremony. In time, though, they grew to care and respect one another and their marriages endured a lifetime."

"Chelsea, get in the real world. It doesn't work that way today. Why would you want to settle for less and miss out on the most beautiful experience of your life? If you choose to settle for anything less, then I'm afraid one day you'll look back on your life with nothing but a heart full of regrets. Then it'll be too late." She patted her arm. "Honey, you'll meet the man you're meant to be with. But if you decide to isolate yourself in a loveless marriage, you'll never have the chance."

Chelsea swallowed hard. "Let's change the subject, Janna. I don't want to talk about this anymore."

"If that's what you want...but please remember what I

said," she quietly replied. "Just promise me that."

"I will." She folded her hands and placed them in her lap. "So tell me, what's going on with Maggie's case? Are there any new details?"

Janna frowned. "I don't feel right having those charges brought against her. She's hurting and I feel like she's being kicked when she's already down. It's making me physically sick inside."

Chelsea was shocked. "I can't believe I'm hearing this from you of all people, Janna. You sound like she's a close friend or something." She frowned. "What's this sudden change of heart really all about?" Her eyes penetrated Janna's. "Something must have happened between last night and now. What's going on?" She pursed her lips.

Janna shrugged her slender shoulders. "I do have a heart and a conscience. I just think that Brant insisted I pursue this for the wrong reasons."

Chelsea's brow furrowed. "What's made you change your mind? Have you personally spoken to Maggie? I thought you couldn't stomach her."

"I never said or implied that. If you think about it, it was always Brant who made the negative comments." Her eyes narrowed. "I don't feel right with preferring charges against her. I always got along well with her whenever Brant and I went out with her and Chris. I feel sorry for her, that's all. She didn't really react any differently than any other woman would have under the circumstances. She was crushed and she lashed out. What was she supposed to do? She'd just learned that the man she loved had cheated on her."

"But she threatened your life. Who knows what she may have done?"

She sighed. "Not quite in the way Brant made it out. He

expounded on what she really said. If anyone else had said what she did, the charges would never fly. And if Brant wasn't Brant Evans, Maggie Allen would have never been arrested."

"Well, she shouldn't have said something that can be misconstrued as a threat," Chelsea insisted.

"I let my emotions get in the way." Janna sighed. "But that's not the only news. There's more."

"What?"

"Brant received his inheritance."

Chelsea's brow puckered. "That's wonderful, but what does that have to do with Maggie?"

"You'll never believe it, Chelsea."

"What?" She grew eager.

She peered into Chelsea's eyes. "Brant leaned that Maggie is his half sister."

Chelsea's mouth dropped open.

****

Brant slowly drove past Chelsea's apartment. He spied Janna's car in the driveway, but Chris's truck wasn't there. "Dammit," he muttered as he continued driving down the tree-lined street. He needed to see her. Why was Janna there? He checked his wristwatch.

He wondered if Nick had delivered the news to Maggie yet. He was dying to see her reaction. Was she as traumatized as he'd been? His animosity toward her grew. He'd never forgive his father for doing this to him. And on top of everything else, the bastard had left her twenty million dollars, the same amount he'd been left. His father could have had the decency to have at least left him more since he'd lived with him as his legitimate child. But no, even in death, he had to rub that bitch into his face. The media would have a field day with this piece of news, especially after the exposé of Maggie's arrest last night. Soon the whole world would know the truth. If there was any consolation, it was the fact that Maggie would be as upset and shaken to learn that he was her baby brother as he had been to learn that she was his older sister.

He pulled into the parking lot of Tom's Diner. He quickly jumped out of the car and then strode to the door. Upon entering, he briefly glanced around. Tom and Maggie sat in a booth. Maggie was holding an envelope in her hand. Nick was standing near them half turned on his heel apparently ready to leave. When the bell on the door tinkled, Nick turned all the way around. Seeing Brant, he motioned to him. Maggie and Tom briefly looked his way, but their expressions gave him no clue as to whether Maggie knew the truth.

Brant slid into a booth near the front of the diner and waited for Nick. "How'd she take the news?" he asked. "Have a seat."

"She hasn't read the letter yet." He checked the time. "I have an appointment. I did inform Maggie, though, that if she has any questions she can contact me." He placed his hands palms down on the table and peered at Brant. "Give her a chance. She seems like a lovely young woman."

He sneered. "Maybe according to my father." He glanced in Maggie's direction. "It looks like I'm just in time for the show."

"Brant, don't you think you should give her some privacy? This news is about to change her entire life. She's going to be distraught and confused and you're probably the last person she wants to see right now. Give her the space and time she needs to absorb everything before you talk to her."

"And you don't think this news has evoked the same emotions in me? My life will never be the same either. My father was a lying, cheating bastard." His tone was cold.

Nick laid a hand on his shoulder. "Brant, show her some compassion, for God's sake. No matter how you felt about your father, please try to remember that none of this is her fault."

Brant's mouth twisted into a sinister smile.

"I've know you you're whole life, Brant," Nick continued. "And I used to pray to God that somewhere in your body even a tiny speck of compassion could be found."

"Maybe I've inherited that trait from my dear old Dad."

"Oh, no." Nick emphatically stated. "If your father didn't have compassion, he wouldn't have written that letter to Maggie all those years ago or given her equal inheritance. Your father was a good man no matter what you think. Don't poison the rest of your life by harboring resentment toward him. I'll tell you the story if you're interested, Brant. I'm sure he wouldn't mind my telling you."

Brant shrugged off his remarks. "I have no interest in my father's past. He glanced in Maggie's direction again. "I can't wait to see the look on her face when she learns that I'm her baby brother."

"What are you really trying to prove, Brant? It's time to bury the hatchet. You can't change the past." His jaw tightened. "If you try to then I'm afraid you are the one who's going to end up harmed."

His eyes narrowed. "Well, I don't like it, and I definitely won't accept it."

CHAPTER SIXTEEN

Chris awkwardly sat on the examining table, the thin paper gown straining against his muscular calves.

"When was the last time you had a complete physical, Chris?" Dr. Rosen asked, peering at him over his wire-rimmed glasses.

Chris shrugged. "It's been awhile, I suppose, but since I haven't had any physical problems, I see no reason for a checkup."

Dr. Rosen checked Chris's pulse then grabbed his stethoscope and listened to his heart and lungs. "You need regular checkups. Everything looks good, Chris, but I'm worried about your weight loss. Is everything all right at home and work?"

Chris rubbed his eyes. "I've been under a lot of stress. You've known me most of my life, doc, and I'm sure you've heard about my situation with Chelsea Howard."

"That's none of my business, Chris. People like to talk,

and I take most of what I hear with a grain of salt."

He loudly exhaled. "Well, in this case, the rumors are true. I had a brief affair with Chelsea, and now she's claiming that I've gotten her pregnant."

"You don't think you're the father?"

Chris shook his head. "No, I don't. I'm not trying to say that Chelsea is wild or anything like that, but I have a nagging feeling that someone else is the father and I'm being corralled into a relationship with her that I don't want."

"Is this the reason you came here today, Chris?"

"Yes, I need to be tested for paternity." His face flushed. "I need to know if I am the father or not."

He looked reassuringly at Chris. "Let me explain how the test is performed. With DNA testing we collect your specimen, Chelsea's, and the baby's, and we can have the results in no time."

"How can we test the baby when it isn't due for a few months?"

"Through amniotic fluids."

"What if Chelsea doesn't agree?" he asked clasping his hands tightly together.

Dr. Rosen raised his eyebrows. "You can get an order to force the testing, especially if she's going after you for medical expenses and child support."

Chris swallowed hard. "And this testing is accurate?"

"Yes, Chris. It will conclusively determine whether you are the biological father or not."

****

"I wonder what he wants," Tom asked cautiously watching Brant. He turned his attention back to Maggie when she didn't reply. "What's the matter?" he asked as her complexion suddenly paled to a ghostly white shade.

With trembling hands, she passed the contents of the envelope to him. "Just read this," she hoarsely whispered as her eyes shifted to Brant. Nick Saunders was exiting the diner and Brant was sitting smugly with his hands folded and placed neatly on the table in front of himself.

Tom's eyes almost popped out of their sockets. "This check is for over twenty million dollars and it's made out to you!" he exclaimed.

She numbly nodded. "Read the letter," she said in a strangled voice. She watched Tom's reaction for a few seconds as she sat in stony silence, her eyes shifting from Tom to Brant and back again.

When Tom was finished, he neatly folded the letter and placed it and the check back into the envelope. "Wow! I don't know what to say, Maggie. I'm flabbergasted."

"Imagine my feelings," she mumbled. "How could my mother have kept this secret her entire life? I wonder if Brant ever knew. Maybe that's why he's harbored so much animosity toward me."

"But don't you think if he'd known he would have tried to use your successes to his advantage somehow?"

"Knowing Brant, I wouldn't put it past him. But how can Brant Evans of all the people on this planet be my brother? How cruel can fate be?"

"I guess you're about to find out." Tom motioned to her with his eyes.

She looked up in time to see Brant making his way over to the booth. She watched in silence until he was towering over her. Her voice froze in her throat. All the questions she needed answers to refused to be asked. The man who was determined to destroy her life was her brother. Brant Evans shared some of the same blood that coursed through her own veins. She was in a state of shock. This new nightmare couldn't truly be reality. She certainly must be losing her mind! That was the answer. So much had happened over the past few days that her mind had finally snapped. She'd wake up soon from this horrible nightmare. She had to.

"Let me help Shelly get ready to close up." Tom pulled himself to his feet. "Brant, please sit down. You two must have a million things to discuss."

Brant slipped into the seat across from Maggie. "I see that you've received the check and read the letter my father left for you." His voice was strained but controlled.

She lifted her eyes. "Did you see the letter?"

"No. I didn't know he'd written one until Nick mentioned it."

She nodded staring down at the table. Her hands were gripped tightly together. She hoped that Brant wouldn't notice how badly she was shaking. She didn't want him to see how unnerved she was. If he did, then she was certain he'd find a way to use it against her.

"If it's any consolation, I never knew either. It looks like dear old Dad pulled the wool over a lot of eyes."

She kept her silence. It wasn't that she had nothing to say. She didn't know where to begin. And even if she did, she wasn't sure that Brant was the man she could trust for the answers. Her head was spinning.

"Did you ever have an inkling about any of this?" he asked.

"No." She swallowed hard. "I need time to digest all of this. I'm not in the mood to talk to you right now, Brant." Her eyes hardened. "Especially under the present circumstances."

"I understand." He stood up. "Just to take some of the pressure off, Maggie, I'm not any happier finding out that you're my sister than you are finding out that I'm your brother."

Looking into his cold hard eyes made her nervousness suddenly leave her. "That's the only truthful thing I think I've ever heard you say. It's probably the only thing the two of us will ever agree on."

He leaned over till his eyes were level with hers. "This new revelation won't change anything as far as the charges Janna has levied against you." He smiled then tipped his hat and left.

Maggie sat frozen in her seat. Tom and Shelly walked over to her.

"Sweet Jesus!" Shelly exclaimed. "Tom told me about your good fortune. Imagine all that money just being handed to you out of the blue!" she squealed. "It's like winning the lottery!"

"What about the other part?" She shifted in her seat. "What about that?"

Shelly scrunched up her face. "Brant for a brother? How can you two be born from the same man and be such total opposites?"

Maggie rubbed her temples. "I feel like I'm in the middle of a nightmare and I'm going to suddenly wake up at any moment. There is no way in hell that this can be real. Maybe I've completely lost my mind and haven't as yet realized it."

Tom put a comforting arm around her shoulder. "Honey, go home and get a good night's sleep. After what you've been through last night, and now with this, I don't know how you can even think clearly about anything."

She picked up the envelope. "I still can't believe that the

man who raised me wasn't really my father. How could my mother have kept that information from me? There are so many questions I'll probably never receive the answers to. If only my parents were alive. I feel so damned deceived." She twisted her hands together. "I was so close to my mother. How could she have made my whole life a lie?"

"Mag, we're here for you whenever you need to talk. Eventually I hope you will find all the answers, but until you do, you'll just have to come to terms with the information you have on hand," Shelly reasoned. "But look at the bright side."

"What's that?"

"You're no longer poor. Now you can afford some of the things you've had to deprive yourself of."

"That's true, but the funny thing is, outside of finding a better place to live, there's nothing else I really care for. I'm contented without all of the material possessions I used to own. I love my simpler, uncomplicated lifestyle. I've never felt freer."

"You'll probably be giving up your job now, though, and I certainly will understand," Tom said. "But I'll sure as hell miss you around here."

"No way! You can't get rid of me that easily. I love it here, and I'd miss the chatting every day with you, Shell, and the regulars. I intend to stay put. You two are my family."

Shelly grabbed her hands. "I'm so happy for you! It's just a shame that Brant has to be connected to it."

She laughed. "He's like a chain around my neck. For the rest of my life I'm going to be connected to Brant Evans." She shuddered. "Imagine the odds of that happening!"

"It still could be worse," Tom reminded her.

Maggie and Shelly raised their eyes to his.

151

He chuckled. "Well, look at it this way. You could have been stuck with Brant for a brother without the twenty million bucks!"

Maggie threw her head back and laughed. "What would I do without you two?"

****

Chris finished his beer and ordered another. He shoved a few coins into the jukebox and then tried to lose himself in the tune. It was no use. His life was ruined and there was nothing he could do about it. He couldn't make Maggie talk to him. She'd never forgive him for what he'd done, and he didn't blame her.

"How's it going, Chris?" Bill Jenson, a foreman on the construction site asked, plopping his large frame on a barstool next to him. "Can I buy you a beer? You look like you've lost your last friend."

Chris ran his hand over his chin. "Yeah, that's how I feel. It's been rough going."

Bill propped his elbows on the bar. "It's none of my business, but me and a few of the guys have noticed you haven't been yourself lately. Is there anything you want to talk about?"

Chris shook his head. "No, Bill. The fix I got myself into only I can get myself out of."

Bill motioned to the bartender who hurried over and set two beers in front of them. "She still won't talk to you?"

"Who?"

"Come on, Chris. You've been wearing your heart on your sleeve. Remember, I was there when Maggie came to the site." He took his baseball cap off and laid it on the bar absentmindedly playing with the rim. "Maggie's a good woman. Give her some time."

Chris looked into Bill's friendly eyes. "She is and she deserves so much more than I gave her. I was a damned fool."

"We know you got hooked, then reeled in by Chelsea Howard. We're not blind." He put his hand up. "I don't mean that you couldn't have gone after her and won her on your own if you had really wanted her. It's just that we saw how everything was coming down. We know what Brant Evans is capable of."

Chris shifted his weight on the barstool. "I wish I could blame Brant for this whole mess, but the truth is that not even Brant forced me to cheat on Maggie. It was my own weakness."

"You're only human. You didn't do anything that most red-blooded men wouldn't have if the opportunity was thrown in their faces."

Chris eyed him. "I know how much you love your wife, Bill. Would you have opted for a one night-stand with someone at the risk of losing her? Think about it for a minute."

He scratched his head, then took a swallow of his beer. He wiped his mouth on the back of his hand. "I don't believe I would. I'm not a risk taker, and I wouldn't risk what my wife and I built up for a fling." He took another swallow of beer. "But then, I wasn't there and I don't know everything that was said or done to lead up to it. Besides, you're not married. Quit beating yourself up. Like I said, you're only human. You're not the first man who ever cheated, and I'm sure you won't be the last."

"That gives me cold comfort at this point. Especially since Chelsea is expecting a baby." He finished his beer and picked up the one Bill had bought him. "Sometimes I wish I could just pack up, get the hell out of Cedar Pines, and start fresh somewhere all over again."

Bill slapped him on the back. "I can't say I know how you feel, buddy, but what I can say is I'm here if you ever need to talk. As far as Maggie is concerned, though, she's worth chasing. Don't give up."

"I know. I just need to find a way to get her to sit down and listen to me. I would give my life for her right now if I had to. Nothing is too good for her."

"I'm sure in time she'll listen to what you have to say."

"I don't think so. Chelsea's pregnancy has made matters even worse than they were."

Bill toyed with his beer bottle. "Just a piece of advice. Get a paternity test and make sure the baby really is yours before you commit to anything with her. I had a buddy who went through the same thing and he didn't find out that the kid wasn't his until a couple of years after he'd married the mother. It was a mess."

"I have. Tomorrow I'm telling Chelsea that she needs to have the baby and herself tested. I refuse to marry Chelsea in any event, but I won't give that child my name if it isn't mine." He looked at Bill. "You know, it's kind of funny in a sick sort of way, but everything I've always wanted, Chelsea is willing to give me. The problem is she's the wrong woman. If I would have found out that *Maggie* was carrying my baby, I would have shouted it from the rooftops."

"Let me get us another round," Bill offered. "If it is your baby, Chris, how do you think Maggie will respond to you? How will you respond to your child?"

Chris stared into his beer bottle as he pondered Bill's questions.

CHAPTER SEVENTEEN

Chelsea closed her eyes wishing she could erase the past year from her mind. How had she allowed herself to get into this situation? When had she become such a conniving non-moralistic human being? Sometimes she even seemed like a stranger to herself, a stranger she was beginning to dislike very much. This wasn't the real person inside of her. Sure, she'd always been a party girl but never at anyone else's expense. All of the values she'd held so highly and expected from everyone else, she now had broken. She knew the consequences of her actions wouldn't leave her unscathed. The truth always had a way of coming out, and when hers did, so many innocent lives would be affected.

She didn't know how much longer she could emotionally carry on this deception without cracking. How many more lives would be destroyed adding to those already destroyed? Why had she allowed herself to be put under Brant Evans' spell, only to be used by him as he'd used so many others in his selfish quest to control everyone he met? What kind of woman would sleep with her best friend's husband? She was worse than a woman who slept with a married man.

This was Janna's husband. Janna and she had been friends forever it seemed, long before Brant Evans had come into the picture. Why had she thought Brant was more important than the trust she and Janna shared as best friends? They'd become closer than most sisters. She'd broken the most important bond two friends shared.

How would she ever be able to face Janna if Janna ever found out the truth? Her life would be over. She'd lose Janna's friendship, and she knew that Brant would never stand by her and their child. She would be left alone to raise the child on her own without any support from him. She would disappear and have her baby. It would be a clean break. That would let Chris off the hook, and he'd be free to go back to his precious Maggie. She had no right to force Chris into this relationship. He was an innocent victim in Brant's scheme.

She never would have seduced Chris if Brant hadn't convinced her to do it. She certainly wasn't attracted to Chris and wasn't interested in him in a sexual way. He was kind and good looking, but his age turned her off. Brant made her feel like a prostitute and he was her pimp. If he'd cared even a little about her, then he certainly wouldn't have wanted her sleeping with another man, especially a man her own father's age. Why had it taken her so long to fully open her eyes and realize this? Why had she allowed herself to be taken in by him?

She was aware that in the beginning her feelings for Brant overshadowed her common sense. The years she and Janna had shared went out the window when she was with him. He had a charismatic, magnetic hold on her heart. After the first few times with him, she justified the affair as just a brief fling that would soon end. No one would be hurt and maybe even in some small way, Brant's affair with her might even strengthen his own marriage. At least that's what Brant had convinced her of in his own sick, self-centered way.

She'd always known that Janna was straitlaced and would blush and become embarrassed at even the tamest off-color jokes. They'd discussed from time to time their sexual fantasies and had even rented movies a few times. But Janna would adamantly refuse to believe that couples would ever even think of doing some of the disgusting, in her opinion, acts that she saw portrayed on the screen. Chelsea would laugh and describe in vivid detail one or two of her own sexual encounters turning Janna's red face even redder.

The first time she slept with Brant, she knew he was craving the wild side of lovemaking. He was an insatiable man with very peculiar, almost bordering on violent, desires as to what he expected to do to a woman's body and what he wanted done to his. Looking at him, she never would have dreamed that he had such a kinky side to him. There was no way Janna would even attempt to try some of the things she and Brant enjoyed. Chelsea relished their adventures in bed, knowing that outside of bed they could only appear as friends. Sometimes, though, she would look at Janna and wonder what Janna would think if she saw the two of them together.

Then the day had come where the guilt set in like a heavy fog, and she knew she had to end the relationship with Brant or her friendship with Janna. She was torn and couldn't live the lie any longer. Try as hard as she could, though, she couldn't end the affair or the friendship. She'd fallen in love with Brant and loved Janna like a sister. Brant became a disease coursing through her veins, eating away at her. Seeing him every day at the police station and sometimes sneaking in the back of the patrol car for a quickie made her ties to him even stronger. Everything would have continued that way if she hadn't discovered one day that she was pregnant. She was carrying Brant's baby. She hadn't been with another man since they'd begun their affair.

Now the decision had been made, at least as far as she was concerned. There was no other way. She would have to end her friendship with Janna, Brant would seek a divorce from Janna, and then she and Brant would be free to marry and raise their baby together. She knew the news would shock him at first, but she never prepared herself for the harsh reaction he would have.

Instead of being swept into his arms with his promises of love and devotion to her and their baby, he instead insisted she get an abortion. She refused. He'd angrily paced back and forth across her floor for such a long time that she was certain he'd wear a hole in the carpet. He only stopped long enough to rant and rave at her like a madman, belittling her with cruel names and insinuations. He blamed her for trapping him, and he refused to take any responsibility.

She was crushed. Because she still loved him so deeply and assumed he would change his mind once his child was born, she'd agreed to go along with his plan to have her seduce Chris Jacoby. She knew he hated Maggie Allen and this was his chance to seek revenge against her for what haunted him, but he'd never told Chelsea what that was. All she knew was that Maggie Allen was partially responsible for Brant's unhappiness and bitterness. He'd told her that much but would relinquish nothing more.

Now she didn't know which way to turn. Brant's plan

was ridiculous and obviously wasn't turning out the way it was intended. Chris didn't fall all over her because she was young and beautiful, but instead avoided her as much as he possibly could. Brant was the only one who would come out a winner. Janna would never find out, and he and Chelsea could continue their affair as they'd been doing. Brant had it all mapped out, but he was the only one who was reaping the benefits.

Chelsea's own life was in a shambles as well as Chris's and Maggie's. No, she had to come clean no matter what the consequences. She had to purge herself of Brant once and for all. She would hatch her own plan of revenge, a devious plan that would totally blow Brant's mind. He thought she was nothing more than a cheap, airheaded blond. Revenge truly would be sweet. She smiled as she concocted the perfect way to show Brant that he had to pay for what he'd done.

CHAPTER EIGHTEEN

Maggie stared at the check. She couldn't believe her eyes. In a matter of seconds, she'd gone from poor and struggling just to meet her basic needs to wealthy enough not to worry about money for the rest of her life. Why was life so strange and unpredictable? How could something horrible and wonderful take place at the same time? Why had her life revolved around so many lies? How could her mother have lived with this deceit and made a lie out of her own life for all these years?

For the first time in her life, Maggie suddenly felt sorry for her father. Well, the man she had presumed was her father. Had he known about the consequences of his daughter's conception? Was that the reason he'd been so cold and distant to her? Was she an appalling reminder of her mother's own dishonesty?

Her mind was whirling with questions she doubted she'd ever find the answers to. The only people who could truthfully answer those questions were dead. If Roger Evans in fact was her father, then how had her mother and him kept their secret all these years, and most importantly, *why* had they kept the secret? Roger had never been a part of her life. In fact, she'd never met the man, but just the same, he'd left her over twenty million dollars. Was that his way of making up to her for his part in her life of lies? Was he easing his conscience for abandoning her and her mother all those years ago?

What about her mother? How was she able to live in the same city with the man who'd gotten her pregnant and then deserted her? Why hadn't they married? There was more to the story. She needed some answers, and her weary mind would get no rest until she received some. The only man who might be able to answer some of her disturbing questions was Nick Saunders.

She pulled Nick's card from the envelope, then picked up the phone and hurriedly dialed his number before she lost her nerve.

"Hello?" His deep voice answered.

"Yes, hello, Mr. Saunders. This is Maggie Allen," she nervously replied.

"Hello, Maggie, and please call me Nick. I thought I might be hearing from you. How can I help you?"

Maggie relaxed a little with the friendliness of his voice. "I don't know where to begin. There's so much I don't understand." She pushed her hair from her forehead. "My mother and Roger Evans I assume were lovers at one time."

"Maggie, I was a personal friend of Roger Evans for most of my life. I'll be happy to answer all of your questions to the best of my ability. Could I come over, or would you rather meet at my office?"

"I think I'd feel more comfortable if you could come to my

home." She gave him her address.

"I'll see you in half an hour then."

Maggie hung up the phone and then put a fresh pot of coffee on. She went to the bathroom, splashed water on her face, and gently dabbed it dry. She ran a comb through her hair and then applied some lipstick.

****

Forty-five minutes later, Nick Saunders was sitting across from her at her small kitchen table, a steaming mug of coffee in front of him.

"I know this has been a lot for you to absorb in such a short period of time."

She nodded. "I'm still numb, completely stunned. It's no bombshell to anyone that Brant and I don't get along very well. Now to find out he's my brother; a brother I never knew existed." She twisted her fingers together. "I'm not even certain I want to know the details, but I feel I must. Does that make any sense to you?"

"I know how complicated it must be for you right now." He reached across the table and gave her hand a friendly pat. "Roger, your father, was very proud of your accomplishments, Maggie. He was frustrated that he couldn't shout it to the world that he was your father. Instead he was forced to stay in the background of your life, never sharing his true feelings about you to anyone but me." He smiled. "I've never seen a man prouder of one of his children and at the same time heartbroken that he had to keep your true parentage hidden."

He pulled a thick book from his leather briefcase, set it on the table, and pushed it toward her. "Open it and it'll prove to you what I've just said. Please don't judge him too harshly. He loved you enough to protect you."

She quizzically met his eyes then looked down at the

162

book, carefully opening it. Hundreds of clippings were neatly organized in protective plastic coating, chronologically by year. She slowly flipped through the pages, seeing her face as an eager seventeen-year-old high school student winning an award for the debating team to her final accomplishment as an executive. Her eyes misted. "I can't believe this."

"I told you he was proud of you. He saved everything that even remotely mentioned your name." He chuckled. "Sometimes he'd even round me up to sit with him in the back of the auditorium when you were giving a speech. He looked as though he'd burst with pride, and I felt sorry for him that he couldn't share the special moment with his friends, especially you, his daughter...but only with me. But never doubt that this man cared deeply for you, Maggie. I can attest to that fact."

Maggie swallowed hard. "Why didn't he make an attempt to see me in all these years? Why didn't he and my mother raise me together? Did he abandon my mother when she became pregnant with me?" Her eyes searched his.

"He wanted to be a part of your life, Maggie. He loved your mother very much, but unfortunately there were barriers as to why they didn't marry."

"What were those barriers?" Her voice trembled. "I need to know. Please tell me everything."

He nodded. "Your father wanted you to know everything if you should ask. Did you read his letter?"

She sniffed. "Yes, it was beautiful. It touched my heart, but it didn't answer any of these questions...only his sincere love for me." She blinked. "I can't believe my mother kept this secret from me for all these years. Why did she do that to me?"

"Let me try to explain. When I'm finished I think you'll understand why your mother never wanted you to find out the truth."

"Did you also know my mother?"

"Yes. She was a beautiful young woman when Roger first met her, and it was no surprise that he fell in love with her. It was obvious to everyone who was close to them that she loved him just as deeply."

Maggie frowned. "Then what happened to keep them apart? It sounds like a tragic romance."

Nick leaned back in his chair. "It ended tragically." A pensive look crossed his face. "Roger had never intended to become so smitten with your mother. It was quite a surprise to him and to me when he professed his undying love for her." He sighed. "But unfortunately, Roger had neglected to share an important detail of his life with her. He never wanted to hurt her, and that was the last thing he'd ever expected to do."

"He obviously did hurt her," Maggie interrupted. "He got her pregnant and then abandoned her, didn't he?" She suddenly felt sorry for her mother. She could only imagine how frightened and alone her mother must have felt not knowing which way to turn. "If he cared so deeply for her as you say he did, then why didn't he do the respectable thing and marry her? None of this is making any sense to me so far."

"It will, Maggie. Roger was a good man, but he did have his faults, and he'd be the first one to tell you that." His brows knitted tightly together. "One of those faults was that his love for your mother prevented him from telling her that he was already married to someone else. We'd discussed that issue several times, but he feared losing her if she were to find out."

Maggie's hand flew to her mouth. "How could he have deceived her like that?"

"I'm not defending what he did. He was wrong, and his deception caused him to lose the only woman he ever truly loved. He'd planned to divorce his wife, Brant's mother, but your mother didn't want to risk being dragged into a nasty divorce proceeding. She did what she felt best for everyone concerned at the time. She did the only thing she could think to do in her situation." He took a sip of his coffee, then slowly set his cup down.

"My mother must have met my father shortly after that, then. To save face she could let him assume that he was my biological father and no one would be the wiser."

"It wasn't quite that way. Your mother was dating your father at the same time she was seeing Roger. Your father was in the military stationed overseas, and she was overwhelmed with loneliness. Roger and your mother were both guilty of cheating, and they both paid the price by not being able to be with one another."

Maggie's face grew warm. "So the man I've believed to be my father all these years was just a convenience when she became pregnant by Roger Evans. I can't believe it!" Her emotions shifted from sympathy for her mother to anger at her for deceiving the two people she'd always professed meant more to her than anything in the world.

"Maggie, your mother loved Sam Allen very much. She was torn between him and Roger. No one but her, though, will ever know what was in her heart for both men. I can only tell you what happened and my perception of events at that time. Neither your mother or Roger planned to fall in love, it happened and was something neither of them could deny." He carefully eyed her. "We all know how those emotions come upon us as quickly as the next blink of our eye."

"Why didn't Roger divorce his wife? He could have found some way to keep my mother out of the legal proceedings."

"Times were different then, Maggie. Jane Evans would have done anything in her power to smear your mother's name through the mud. She would have eventually learned the truth, and your mother's reputation would have been destroyed. It was disgrace enough to have a child out of wedlock, but worse to be carrying a married man's child."

She ran her hand through her hair. "They could have found a way if they'd both wanted it badly enough. They could have moved away from here and started a life somewhere else where no one knew them."

"No, they couldn't. Jane Evans was a cold, bitter, vindictive woman. For spite, she would have made life miserable for them no matter where they went, even if things had worked out and they did eventually marry. They wouldn't have had a moment's peace."

She drummed her fingers on the tabletop. "Wouldn't she have been justified in her feelings? After all, she was the scorned woman. He couldn't have been that unhappy with Jane. Three years after my birth, he had a child — Brant — with her."

"Believe me, Maggie, Brant was not conceived out of love. After Roger lost your mother, he began drinking and womanizing. He'd lost the only woman he ever truly loved. He didn't care anymore. The light went out of his life."

"But the man who raised me as my father was basically used only as a convenience for my mother to save face. It wasn't right to do that to him or any man."

"No, Maggie, don't ever think that. I told you that your mother loved Sam very much. This may sound preposterous, but I think in time she actually convinced herself that Sam truly was your biological father."

She chewed her bottom lip. "This is so difficult to digest.

Roger Evans and my mother parted ways for good then?"

He nodded. "Roger tried to see your mother a few times and tried to give her money for your support, but she refused. He begged her to meet him at the park just so he could see what his daughter looked like. She wouldn't relent, and finally, because of the love he still carried for her, he agreed to step back into the shadows and let Sam Allen take over the role he so desperately craved to fill. I want you to know, Maggie, that he went to his grave still loving your mother."

"This whole story is so sad and tragic." She let her breath out in a rush and then looked at Nick with pained eyes. "I don't know what to think."

"Maggie, I realize how much this news has turned your life upside down in more ways than one." He gazed into her eyes. "Just take your time to absorb everything. Remember that I'll answer any questions that may come to mind." He patted her hand. "That letter Roger wrote to you was written shortly before his death. He wanted you to know how he felt about you...how he'd always felt about you."

"May I keep these clippings for a while?"

"They're yours to do with what you want." He smiled. "He was proud of you and so disappointed that he couldn't share your accomplishments with you."

"Thank you, Nick." She picked up the folder and held it to her chest.

CHAPTER NINETEEN

Maggie beamed as she laid a hand on Shelly's arm. "Are the boys all set for our trip to the zoo?"

"They're excited beyond belief that you're going with us. Every day they ask me if it's the day." She giggled.

"I'm looking forward to it as much as they are. You know how much fun I have with the boys." Her face grew serious. "I want the day to be on me. No matter what they want."

Shelly emphatically shook her head back and forth. "Mag, I can't let you do that. This outing is our treat to you."

Maggie stared hard at her. "I want to do this, Shelly. What good is having all of this money if I can't spend some of it on those I love?"

Shelly hugged her. "You are the sweetest person I've ever known," she answered in a choked voice.

Tom stood at the counter grinning at the two women. "Okay, you two," he laughed. "Later I'll get the violin players in here, but for now how about we get the grill fired up before the hungry crowd starts stampeding in."

Shelly grabbed an apron and tied it around her waist as Maggie prepared to brew the coffee. A light rapping on the glass caused the three of them to turn and look in the direction of the door.

"Wonder who that is?" Tom asked. "We don't open for fifteen more minutes." He strode to the door. He cupped his hands over his eyes and peered out into the darkness, then turned and shot a glance in Maggie's direction. "It's Brant," he loudly whispered, unlocking the door at the same time.

Brant pushed through the door and rushed over to where Maggie stood. "Got a minute, Maggie?"

She sharply eyed him. "What do you want, Brant?"

He shifted his weight from one foot to the other. "Can I talk to you privately?"

"What is it, Brant?" Her tone of voice was less than civil. "I have work to do."

He cocked an eye. "I must say that I'm surprised you're still working here after your sudden good fortune."

"I don't have all day, Brant. What do you want? I'm sure you didn't come here to invite me to a family reunion."

He laughed at her sarcasm. "Actually, I'm here on behalf of Janna." His jaw tightened. "I'll get right to the point."

"Please do."

"Janna has agreed to drop the charges if you issue her a formal apology."

"What?" Her mouth dropped open. "I can't believe you had the nerve to come here and ask me that."

"Janna and I talked it out last night, and we decided that under the present circumstances surrounding our — yours and my — biological father, she should think about dismissing the charges. Frankly, none of us wants the publicity. God only knows how we'll be hounded once the story gets out. Janna and I still feel that an apology from you is in order though." He shrugged his muscular shoulders. "Then we can all get on with our lives. I think this is a generous offer."

Maggie threw her head back and laughed. "This is too much. You can tell Janna that I said no deal. I'm not in the habit of apologizing for something I never did, and I don't intend to start."

His lips tightened. "Then I guess we'll see you in court. The media will have a field day with this." He tipped his hat to her. "But at least you now have the means to pay for an attorney, *Sis*."

Maggie placed her hands on her hips. She was livid but kept her retort to herself.

****

Chris sat in his truck staring at the desolate construction site. As soon as he finished work today, he would confront Chelsea about getting the DNA testing. He still intended to pack his things and move out tonight in any event.

He ran his hand over his jaw. He'd figure out a way to get Maggie to talk to him again. Maybe she'd even decide someday to give him another chance. All he had to do was convince her that he'd always loved her and only her and spend the rest of his life making it up to her. He knew she wouldn't be receptive to him for a long time, but he'd wait. All he could do was wait. He couldn't imagine the rest of his life without Maggie. He had to get her back. He would grovel if he had to. Pride didn't matter to him anymore. He was nothing without her.

A truck pulled up next to his. Four of his crew jumped out and headed in his direction. He wished he had half the energy these men had. He had to admit he had one hell of a crew and was grateful that he'd signed them on. They were loyal and showed him proper respect, but were also his best friends.

He grabbed his thermos of coffee and slid out of the truck.

****

Chelsea lay on her bed staring up at the ceiling. She wished Brant would come over. She missed him. He barely gave her the time of day anymore. There was so much going on in his life right now, but it still didn't give him an excuse to ignore her. Janna had said that he'd gone ballistic when he learned that Maggie Allen was his sister. She laughed out loud. How ironic. The one person he most despised in this world turned out to be his half-sister.

Brant made her angry, though, with his lack of consideration or concern for her and their child's well-being. It was only a matter of time before Chris learned the truth about the baby, and when he did, all hell would break lose. It served Brant right. Why should he be the one to always come out on top? She was tired of being used by him. Her hormones were driving her crazy today even more than usual. She had to eventually come clean with what she'd done. Her conscience no longer allowed her to betray and hurt Janna, or for that matter Chris. The guilt she carried inside was eating her up.

Chelsea glanced at the bedside clock, then forced herself to get up. She wriggled her feet into her bedroom slippers, padded to the bathroom, and splashed cold water on her face. She patted her face dry, then looked into the mirror noticing the puffiness under her eyes. She was restless and bored. Brant had talked her into taking a leave of absence until after the baby was born. She missed seeing him every day and often wondered if he wanted her out of the way so he wouldn't have to constantly be reminded of her pregnancy. She worried that the pregnancy would ruin her figure for good. She'd seen women who'd never been able to shed the unwanted pounds after giving birth and even worse, those that had been left with ugly stretch marks and sagging skin that refused to be toned no matter what exercises they did.

She touched her stomach. What type of mother would she be to this little stranger she was carrying inside of her? She tried to muster the maternal emotions she knew she should be feeling, but at times the whole idea of being a mother annoyed her. This child would tie her down. She didn't know if she was ready to be a mother, but worse, if she even *wanted* to be a mother. Even if Chris had without question gone along with everything, married her, and settled into the role of husband and father, could she have settled into the role of wife and mother? Then at other times, unexpectedly and right out of the blue, she'd be struck with a nostalgic bonding with this unborn child growing within her and become overwhelmed and excited with the prospect of motherhood. She would be overcome with powerful emotions of wanting to protect and defend her child from this cruel, cold world.

She had no right to disrupt Chris's life, but she had disrupted it in the cruelest way possible. And very soon, he would find out the truth. Once she took the test, he would know the baby wasn't his. Tongues would be wagging with everyone wondering who the father was. What would they all think if they knew Brant Evans was the father? His world would be turned upside down with no way to escape the truth. It would serve him right. He wanted to have his cake and eat it too. Did he think she would settle for being his mistress forever?

The tiny apartment stifled her. It was too small, almost

making her claustrophobic. She didn't have any hobbies to occupy the lonely hours, even if she had the space to partake of any. Cooking wasn't her forté so she spent most days, when Janna was unavailable, reading her fashion magazines or watching cop shows on TV. She was fascinated with the law but realized that most times she found herself on the side of the perpetrator instead of where her loyalty should lie, with truth and honesty. Brant had tainted her faith in the justice system. She learned very soon that everyone had a price, and favors didn't necessarily have to involve money.

She walked into the compact kitchen-dining area and over to the refrigerator. She poured herself a glass of milk and gulped it down. She set the glass in the sink and walked to the living room. She peered out of the window. It was going to be another scorcher. The blazing sun was high in the clear blue sky without a cloud in sight. This part of pregnancy she despised. She felt isolated and disconnected from everyone around her. As her body grew heavy and her weight became uncomfortable, she became even more miserable. Her feet swelled so badly that for days on end she couldn't even squeeze them into her shoes.

In the numerous made-for-TV movies she watched, the women and their partners or husbands rejoiced and anxiously awaited the blessed event, but in her life there was no celebration. She felt cheated. Brant had cheated her, and she had cheated Chris and Maggie. Things were coming full circle, and she understood the meaning of "what goes around comes around". But it still didn't give her much satisfaction, because it seemed that Brant always managed to escape getting his just due.

She plopped down on the sofa and flicked on the TV. A

few minutes later, she heard the familiar tapping on the door. A smile broke across her face as she ran to it. "I didn't expect you, honey," she said after making certain Brant was alone. "I was hoping you'd stop by. I've missed you."

He silently slipped inside. "Are you alone?"

She laughed. "Of course I am. Who do you think would be here?"

He shrugged. "Just being careful. We have to watch every move we make." He looked sharply at her. "The only reason no one suspects my frequent visits is because they know you are a close friend of Janna and me. They think I'm just popping in from time to time to make sure you're okay since the father of your child is uncaring."

"I'm always cautious." She smiled brightly. "I'm so happy you showed up. I've been feeling especially lonely today. It's been rough." She twisted her hands together. "Chris is insisting that the baby and I be tested." She waited for Brant's reaction as she brushed her blond hair from her brow. "I think he's already talked to a doctor."

Brant's eyes flashed. "You can't get the DNA testing done on the baby!" he stormed.

Chelsea paced back and forth across the living room floor. "What am I supposed to do, Brant?" she wined. "I can't stop him from determining paternity. What if he gets a court order?"

His eyes smoldered making them even darker than they already were. "He can't. It's as simple as that. You've got to come up with a plan to convince him beyond a shadow of a doubt that the baby is his without his wanting a test to prove it. At least stall him until after you're married and the baby is born."

She stopped pacing and stood in front of Brant, placing

174

her hands on his firm chest. "I can't. He wants nothing to do with me. I told you he's not as stupid as you thought he was. He won't marry me until I have the test."

His jaw twitched. "Dammit! We've got to figure something out. Just find some way to stall him for a while longer. Come on, you're a smart girl, Chelsea. Use your charms on him."

Her eyes widened. "How? I've tried every trick in the book and he's not falling for any of it. He's demanding the test. We have too much technology at our disposal today, Brant. It's only a matter of time before this blows up in our faces! There's no way he's going to wait until the baby is born."

He grabbed her wrists. "There has to be a way...short of killing him."

Chelsea shivered even with the stifling heat inside the apartment. "Brant, you wouldn't..."

He shot her a disgusted look then released her wrists. "I'm just talking off the top of my head."

She wasn't convinced. His rigid jaw and the way he clenched and unclenched his fists frightened her. "Honey, why don't you and I just get the hell out of Cedar Point? We can raise our child together. It's the only way." Her eyes brightened at the thought. "We love each other and should be together. We can begin a brand new life."

Brant scoffed. "What do you propose we live on?'

"You've received your inheritance."

He shot her a questioning look.

"Janna told me."

"I suppose she told you the rest."

She nodded. "It's unbelievable! But anyway, you have the money so that isn't a problem. We can just pack up and leave. Don't do to our baby what your father did to Maggie. I want our child to know who his or her daddy is."

His eyes narrowed. "Oh, I'm supposed to leave my job, the city where I was born and raised, and just disappear with you and start life over? Is that what you're proposing?"

Her usually bright eyes clouded. "Yes, Brant. You and me and our baby can be a family."

He mockingly laughed at her. "Get that idea out of that pretty head of yours. You and I will never be married, and the baby you're carrying will never have my name."

"But, honey, I love you," she pouted. "I thought you loved me too."

He smirked. "Chelsea, have I ever led you to believe that I loved you or wanted to spend my life with you?" He pointed a finger at her. "No, I didn't. Do you want to know why? Or should I spell it out for you?"

Her bottom lip trembled.

"I don't love you, Chelsea. I never have and never will."

Her eyes teared. "You do, Brant. I know you do. The way we make love proves it. You're just upset about finding out that Maggie Allen is your sister. Don't say such cruel things to me."

"Oh yes, I am upset about that piece of news, but you've got it wrong, baby, about you and me. You practically threw yourself at me." He shrugged. "I took what you offered. Any red-blooded man would have done the same thing. Given enough time, even Janna would agree that you are nothing but a tease and a gold digger."

"You...you used me," she choked. Tears spilled from her eyes. "You bastard! You'll never get away with this! I swear to God you'll get yours," she sputtered. "I'll tell Chris and Janna everything. I'm sure Janna will be grateful to learn what a *faithful, loving husband* you've been!"

He grunted. "Calm down. You're not going to say anything to anyone. If you do, you and that bastard you're carrying will be sorry." His voice was stone cold. "Furthermore, what right do you have to judge me after what you've done to your best friend?"

"I can't believe you're saying these terrible things to me, Brant! How can you call the child we created together out of our love a bastard? It's your own flesh and blood, for God's sake! Don't you have any feelings for anyone but yourself?"

"You brought this on all by yourself. Never once did I ever say that you and I would have a future together. Did I?" he snapped. "If I were you, I'd think of a way to get Jacoby to marry you as soon as possible. That's your only hope at this point." He shrugged his shoulders. "I honestly don't know what you expect from me."

"I expect you to care." Her bottom lip trembled uncontrollably. "Don't do this to me, Brant. Please, I'm begging you. I'm so scared and alone."

He walked to the door, then turned and gave her a sharp look. He shook his head as he opened the door and slammed it shut behind him.

Chelsea pounded her fists on the sofa. "Damn you, Brant!" she shrieked. She picked up her cell phone and then quickly set it back down. No, she couldn't call Janna just yet. She needed to get proof that even Brant would have no way of disputing. She'd find a way to put him in the hot seat, and she'd strap him in so tightly he'd never escape.

****

Chris stomped into the bedroom, a cardboard box gripped in his large, callused hands. He grabbed his visible items from the top of the dresser and threw them into the box,

177

then walked into the bathroom and seized his toothbrush and shaving supplies from the shelf.

"What are you doing, Chris?"

He whirled around to face Chelsea. "What does it look like? I'm packing my stuff and getting the hell out of here."

"Just like that?" Her bottom lip quivered. She looked down at her bulging stomach. "You're going to walk out on me and the baby."

"Cut the act, Chelsea." He turned back to his task. She sniffled and he squared his shoulders. "The tears and threats aren't going to work this time."

"It's your baby, Chris. I'm not lying to you. Did you get the test?"

He threw his deodorant into the box. "Yes, I did, and you know damned well that you and the baby also need to be tested!"

"How would I know that, Chris? I've never been involved with anything like this before. And I've certainly never been pregnant before."

He let his breath out in a rush. "I told you before that I have no intentions of living with you. I am also going to stop supporting you until I know one way or the other whose baby you're carrying. If it proves to be mine, then I'll do my duty."

Chelsea's lips drew up into a pout. "I could take you to court. I don't want it to come to that, but I could, Chris. You can't walk out on me in my condition and leave me penniless."

Chris tossed the box aside and turned around. "That's a good idea. Why don't you take me to court? The judge will force you to get the test and this mess will be settled once and for all!" He threw his arms up. "Do it, Chelsea! You'd be doing me a big favor!"

She was at a loss for words. "Where are you going to be

staying? What if I need to reach you?"

"I have no idea where I'll be, just as far away from you as I can get!" He picked up his cell phone. "You know how to reach me."

CHAPTER TWENTY

Maggie tousled Terry and Tommy's sandy-brown hair. "So, what do you boys think of those monkeys over there?"

Terry laughed. "I can act like them." He dangled his arms at his sides and spread his legs slightly apart as he hunched his back, then leaned forward making loud grunting sounds.

"Me too!" Tommy excitedly piped up. "Watch me too, Maggie."

"I'm watching," she said with a laugh as Tommy imitated his brother.

"The boys have such a great time with you, Maggie," Shelly said. "I'm glad you came with us today. And thank you for your generosity."

Maggie shielded her eyes against the glaring sun, watching as Terry and Tommy stood in front of the monkeys' cage. "They're precious." She patted Shelly's shoulder. "Being with them is the most fun that I've had in quite a while. It feels good to forget about everything else and just enjoy life for a change."

"They've been talking about this all week. You have a special way with kids, Maggie."

"You have a couple of special little guys."

"Thanks," she proudly answered.

They sat on a bench as the boys played nearby. "I'm glad today turned out to be such a beautiful day."

Shelly nodded. "I was so afraid it was going to rain. The boys would have been heartbroken."

"Well, if it had rained, we'd have found something else to do. There was no way I was going to give up being with Terry and Tommy today."

Shelly leaned back on the bench. "Mag, can I ask you a personal question?"

"Of course." She peered into Shelly's pleasant face.

"Do you think the boys will turn out okay without a father in their lives?"

"Honey, you're doing a wonderful job with them!" she exclaimed. "They are two very happy, well-adjusted little boys." She studied Shelly's face. "I think you're the one who wants a man around. You're lonely, I can tell. This is really about you, isn't it, Shell?"

She blushed as she stared down at her hands. "Sometimes I do get lonely, especially when the boys are tucked into bed at night. It would be nice to have someone there that I could lean on once in a while. Then I wonder how the boys would react to a man who isn't their father. What if he wasn't as receptive to them either?"

"There are a lot of nice men who would jump at the chance to take you out."

"I don't know about that, but I haven't met anyone who

gives me that spark. Do you know what I mean?"

She nodded. "I know exactly what you mean." She squeezed Shelly's hand. "Someday you'll meet the man who's meant for you and the boys. You're young, honey. You don't need to rush into anything. Someday your Prince Charming will come along and probably when you least expect it."

"Sometimes I doubt the perfect man for me even exists, and I don't know if it would be worth the bother to become involved if he did."

"He does, Shelly. You've got a long life ahead of you, and I don't think you'll be living that life alone. It takes two people to make a relationship, but sometimes you still end up getting hurt. I still believe that it's worse to never have loved at all than to have loved and lost."

She frowned. "Life is so strange. I mean, look at everything that's happened to you, especially finding out that Brant is your half-brother."

"I know. I'm still dealing with that, and it'll take some time for me to understand all the facts surrounding it. But no matter what, it still doesn't change the kind of man Brant Evans is. I am learning about his father and from what I can determine, Brant is the total opposite of him."

"Makes you wonder. It certainly is a small world."

"A small world and much too short a life by the time you finally figure it all out. It's funny how things come into your life, leave, and then come back again. If you're lucky enough, you can even change the outcome the second time around."

"Uh oh, do I detect a little bit of morbid philosophy here?" Shelly asked.

Maggie sighed. "Not at all. I just want to share my newfound wealth and wisdom gained as well. Losing everything I had and moving here was one of the best things that could have happened to me, even if it didn't seem like it at the time. It made me aware of the simple pleasures in life. Working at the diner is one of those pleasures. I really enjoy the joking and laughter every day. I met some wonderful people there. But you and Tom are the best." She tossed her hair. "And now I've been blessed with wealth again. The only difference is that I didn't have to work for it this time."

"Maggie, I can't even picture you in that corporate world. You seem too kind and honest."

She threw her head back and laughed. "Thank you, Shell. I'll accept the compliment." She glanced over at the boys. "Those monkeys sure have them captivated." She inhaled deeply. "Shelly, I've been thinking about something, and I need to run it by you."

"Sure." She smiled. "What's up?"

"You know how Tom's been saving to have the floor retiled and the walls painted in the diner? Well, I want to do that for him."

"Hmmm, that's a very generous offer, Maggie, but you know Tom won't let you do it."

Her eyes glowed. "I thought about that. That's where you come in."

Shelly's eyes brightened as she leaned closer. "What's the plan?"

****

Brant sprawled on his back stretching his tired limbs.

"Are you all right, honey? You tossed and turned all night."

He put an arm around Janna drawing her close. She rested her head on his firm chest. "Yeah, it's just been a rough week." He smiled. "I'm glad for the day off."

183

"What would you like to do?" she asked.

"I think I'd like to just spend the day doing nothing in particular. Maybe I'll take a walk around and get some ideas for the landscaping."

"Doesn't sound very exciting to me."

He laughed. "And what would you rather I do, my love?"

"I thought maybe we could take a ride in the country. Remember that cozy inn we saw out on Highway 98?" Her eyes glowed. "Why don't we spend the night there, Brant? We haven't gotten away together in so long."

"Honey, we just moved into this house. Why would you want to spend the night somewhere else?"

"I love this house, Brant. I just thought it would be nice to get away alone together without any distractions." The beeping of his cell phone interrupted her. "That's what I mean," she said pointing to it. She shook her head as she sat up and grabbed her bathrobe, slipping it over her shoulders. "I'm sure it's some emergency at the station for you," she answered sliding out of bed.

Brant grabbed the phone as Janna strode to the bathroom. "Yeah?" he growled.

"Brant, I need to see you right away!" Chelsea hysterically cried.

"Chelsea, is that you?" he snarled. "What do you want?"

"I need to see you. Chris left me last night."

"Maybe he just had a long night out with the boys. I'm sure he'll return."

"No, Brant. He packed his things and moved out. He's not going to pay for anything! I don't know what to do! I'm scared!"

Brant ran his hand threw his hair. "Hold on a second." He walked to the bathroom door and heard the shower running.

"Calm down. I'll be over in a little while and we'll figure everything out." He ended the call and then pulled on a pair of dress slacks and a polo shirt. He walked into the bathroom and peeked into the shower. "I've got an emergency, honey. I'll be back as soon as I can."

Janna answered with a bar of soap aimed at him. He ducked, narrowly missing being struck in the forehead. "I love you too, honey."

****

Fifteen minutes later Brant stood in Chelsea's tiny living room. He loosened the collar of his shirt. "It's hot in here, Chelsea."

"The air conditioner broke," she wined.

"Well, go get a new one."

"With what?" Her eyes brimmed with tears. "I'm scared, Brant." She covered her face with her hands. "How am I supposed to pay rent and everything?"

Brant was quickly at her side scooping her into his arms. "Shhh," he soothed as he patted her back. "We'll figure something out." He led her to the sofa and then sat next to her. "Tell me exactly what happened."

She sniffed. "Chris said unless I get the baby tested to find out if he's the biological father, he will have nothing to do with me."

Brant's jaw tightened. "Maybe I should pay him a little visit."

"What good will that do?" she cried. "As soon as the results of the test are in, he'll know he's not the father."

"Well, maybe I can persuade him to move back in until the test results are in. You can stall him for a while longer until we can figure everything out. We've already had this discussion."

She threw her hands in the air. "I can't stall him," she shouted. "I've tried everything. Now I have no money, no job...nothing!" She swallowed hard. "You're going to have to help me, Brant."

His eyes slanted. "I don't have to do anything, Chelsea."

"Brant, you're the father of my baby. If I went to court it would be simple to prove."

He roughly grabbed her shoulders. "Don't even think about it! You tricked me by getting pregnant. You should have been on the pill or something."

"I can't believe I'm hearing you correctly, Brant. Since when is this pregnancy all my fault?" She pushed his hands from her shoulders. "Are you willing to take responsibility for this baby?"

He smirked. "Don't threaten me." He stood up. "In fact, don't you ever call me again." He walked to the door then turned and pointed a finger at her. "In fact, don't even come near Janna again either. Stay the hell out of our lives."

She stared at him but kept silent.

"I told you that you should have gotten rid of the little bastard while you had the chance. I'm not going to spend the rest of my life supporting a child I never wanted." He slammed out of the door.

Chelsea walked to the window, watched him speed off, then hurried over to the end table and pressed a button on her cell phone. She picked up her phone and then played it back. Clear as a bell. She smiled smugly. "We'll see, Brant...we'll see."

CHAPTER TWENTY-ONE

Maggie stood gazing at the graves. Her parents' monumental headstone, which was shared between them, glistened in the setting sun, casting an eerie shadow over the graves. She gently ran her hand over the headstone carefully reading each word inscribed, then solemnly walked to her mother's grave.

"Why, Mom? Why didn't you tell me? I would have forgiven you." She stared at the grassy mound. Was her mother at peace? How could she have taken this horrendous secret to the grave with her? She needed more answers. She needed closure. All three of her parents were dead. She laughed at the irony of her last thought. *Three parents.* She'd had two fathers, but all her life felt as though she had none. She'd never had a paternal bonding with either of them. Sadness gripped her heart.

She moved back to her father's grave and knelt before it. "I'm so sorry," she whispered. "If I'd only known." She wiped tears from her eyes. "I'm sorry that we never got along, but I'm mostly sorry that you and I both lived a lie." She took a shaky breath. "There was no way you ever suspected, was there? Yet, something deep inside of you prevented you from loving me. In a strange way I can understand that now. I just wish you were here now so I could tell you how sorry I am that I never thanked you for giving me the strength to reach my goals. I wanted you to be proud of me...that's all I wanted."

****

Shelly tucked the boys into their beds then kissed their rosy cheeks. "Did you two have a good time today?"

"Yeah!" they answered in unison.

"Maggie's fun!" Tommy said stifling a yawn.

"When can we see her again?" Terry asked.

"Real soon, honey."

Terry hugged her neck and then turned on his side pulling his blanket to his chin.

Tommy smiled up at her. His tongue was wedged in the space where his two front teeth used to live. She bent and kissed his cheek and pulled the blanket he'd already kicked off around his shoulders.

She smiled. "We'll have to go to the zoo again real soon. Go to sleep like good boys." She snapped off the light and tiptoed out of their bedroom.

She ran a bath and spent a leisurely time relaxing in the tub thinking about Maggie's plan to remodel the diner. Tom would be so happy, even though he would protest loudly. But if anyone besides Maggie deserved some happiness and good fortune out of life, it was Tom. She was grateful for all he had done for her and her boys. She couldn't love him more if he'd been her own father. She leaned back letting the soft bubbles massage her breasts as she mapped out her part of Maggie's plan. She needed to make sure she didn't do or say anything to arouse Tom's suspicions, and she knew that would be much easier said than done.

When her bath was finished, she toweled herself dry and threw on a fluffy bathrobe. She shuffled to the kitchen, her large teddy bear slippers swishing across the linoleum floor. She picked up the phone and dialed Tom's number.

"Hello," Tom's drowsy voice answered.

"Hi, it's Shelly, Tom. I'm sorry if I woke you."

"No, Shelly, I was just dozing in my easy chair. Is everything all right? How are the boys?" he worriedly asked.

"Everything is great and the boys are sound asleep. We had a big day at the zoo and they're conked out," she said with a laugh.

"That's right, today was the day. So did you and Maggie have a good time too?"

"Oh, yes! We had as good a time as the boys did. Next time we want you to come with us too."

"I just might." He chuckled.

"The reason I called, Tom, is that I was wondering if you could do me a favor one night this week. I'm not sure what night it is, but I have a meeting at the boys' school. It's a parent thing. The reason I'm asking you to babysit is that since it's a school night I'd like to keep the boys at home so they can go to sleep at their regular bedtime and in their own beds. Besides, I know they'd enjoy spending some time with you." She wondered if she'd spoken too quickly arousing his suspicions.

"I'd love to do it. Just let me know what night." He was silent for a moment. "Shelly?"

"Yes, Tom?"

"Why didn't you wait to ask me tomorrow morning?"

She quickly racked her brain for an appropriate answer. "You know how crazy it gets on Monday mornings. I would have probably forgotten."

He was silent for a moment as though he were pondering her answer. "Okay. Well, I'll see you in the morning, then."

"Night, Tom, and thank you." She clicked the phone off, then quickly punched in Maggie's number. "Hi, Mag. I've got good news. Tom will babysit so just let me know what night the contractors are coming over."

Maggie grinned. "Great! Now all we have to do is figure out a way to occupy Tom for an entire day while the work is being done."

Shelly giggled. "Knowing you, I'm sure you'll come up with something."

"I've always got a plan up my sleeve," Maggie slyly replied.

****

Chelsea steadied her hand then dialed Chris's cell phone number. After three rings, he answered. "Chris, please don't hang up. I need to talk to you."

"There's nothing to talk about, Chelsea." His voice was cold. "Unless you've arranged for the tests."

"Chris, I have some information I need to share with you."

"I'll listen, but it doesn't mean I'll believe anything you have to say," he answered noncommittally.

"This is something I need to tell you face to face, not over the phone," she pleaded. "Please come over as soon as you can."

He frowned. "How do I know you're not setting me up? Quite frankly, I don't trust you, Chelsea."

"Please, Chris. You're the one holding all the cards." She ran a shaky hand through her hair. "Please come over and I'll

190

explain everything to you. This information is going to change your life…and mine. I promise."

He hesitated. "Okay, I can be there in ten minutes, but you'd better not be pulling anything," he warned.

"I swear I'm not, Chris. Thank you."

****

Janna furiously ran the brush through her hair. Her golden mane glistened in the lights surrounding the mirror attached to her dressing table.

"How long do I have to put up with this silent treatment of yours, Janna?" Brant demanded as his eyes met hers in the mirror.

She dropped her eyes. "I have nothing to say, Brant. You never listen to a word I say anyway. In fact, lately you barely listen or seem to care about anything that involves me. We're the epitome of the spoiled, young, rich couple. We have it all, but in the process we've lost one another." She let out a weary sigh. "I never wanted to end up the way my parents did." She laughed, but it was a sad laugh that came from her heart. "The irony is that every day we are becoming more and more like my parents. They went about their individual daily lives and attended the appropriate social functions, but that's all they shared together. Their existence as a happy, rich couple in love was a farce. They never shared a moment together for themselves. At first I thought it was because of their busy social schedules, but as time went on, I realized that they kept themselves busy so they wouldn't have to spend time alone together. Later it became evident that they actually despised one another." She swallowed the lump in her throat. "That's what's happening to us. We're together, but so far apart."

"Oh come on, honey. Aren't you being a bit dramatic?

You know that my job isn't a nine to five. It never has been and never will be. When I get a call, I have to go. I'm a peace officer. You used to be proud of my work. What's changed your mind?"

"I still am proud of what you do, Brant, but your schedule is not exactly the way you state it is. You've been known to request overtime, to work your vacation time and personal days off. You aren't required to do that, you ask for it."

"You're mad at me because I love and enjoy my work?" he incredulously asked.

"No, Brant," she said quietly, carefully choosing her words. "I'm hurt because you don't seem to care whether we spend any time together or not." She set her dainty hairbrush down and then turned facing him. "Name the last time that you and I spent an entire day alone together?"

His eyes shifted. "Come on, honey. Don't be ridiculous."

"You can't," she continued. "The most upsetting part of it is that you don't seem to even care. If I'm angry, that is the reason why, Brant."

He walked over to her. "Janna, that's not true. I love being with you. It's just that I've been under an enormous amount of pressure lately. You know that I have been. Sometimes I can't even think straight." He feebly fought for an explanation.

"You've received your inheritance, Brant, so don't you think, or more to the point, don't you *want* to take some time off to relax and relieve some of the stress you say you're under?"

"Relax!" He raised his eyebrows. "Janna, for Christ's sake, how can you be so damned insensitive to me? Especially now? My life has been ripped apart, and you accuse me of being insensitive to you." His jaw tightened. "You of all people should understand what I'm going through instead of putting me on the defensive." His voice rose with the last word.

"Don't you dare twist this around, Brant," she retorted in a blistering voice. "You've been shutting me out for much too long now. At first I tried to be patient, knowing the news about Maggie had come as a blow because of your negative feelings for her. When I tried to offer my support, you pushed me away. There's an invisible wall between us. I can see you through it, but I can't touch you. Sometimes I don't even think I know you anymore. To be brutally honest, Brant, at those times I'm not even sure I want to know you." She looked into his dark, brooding eyes. "This has been going on long before you found out that Maggie is your sister. Your animosity toward her is eating you alive. Your hatred is rotting your heart."

He thoughtfully rubbed his jaw. "Try to see this from my point of view, Janna. Can't you see what this has done to me?"

"I've been trying to see things from your prospective, but as I've told you before, your vendetta against Maggie Allen isn't healthy. Can't you just leave her alone? She hasn't done anything to you. The circumstances surrounding her birth aren't her fault."

"I've been trying to deal with my feelings toward Maggie. In fact, I even tried to talk to her. I told her you'd be willing to drop the charges if she offered you an apology." He peered at his wife. "She's not the wonderful woman you make her out to be. She turned the offer down flat," he scoffed waiting for Janna's reaction.

Her mouth dropped open as she stared in disbelief at him. "You had no right to talk to her, Brant. Why can't you back off? Enough is enough. I'm *not* going to pursue a court trial, Brant. This whole situation has gotten way out of hand. It's going to end now!"

The forcefulness of her words stunned him. "She threatened your life, dammit, Janna! As your husband, and my sworn duty as an officer of the law, I'm doing my job by protecting you from intended harm." He disgustedly rammed his hands into his pockets. "Now to hear you say that the whole thing is my fault. Why the sudden softening of the heart toward Maggie?" he demanded. "Why are you taking her side against me?"

"This has nothing at all to do with taking sides. You're blowing everything way out of proportion." She touched his shoulder. "Please let go of your anger, Brant, before it destroys not only you, but us." Her lips trembled. "I can't live with your anger anymore. Like it or not, Maggie's your sister and there's nothing you can do about it, so the sooner you begin to accept it the better off we'll all be."

"I can't accept it, Janna!" He removed his hands from his pockets and wildly pointed, making stabbing gestures at the air. "Of all the underhanded things my father could have done, this was the lowest! How could he do this to me?"

"It's not Maggie's fault that she's your father's daughter. She's probably not any happier than you are about the situation. But the truth is that Maggie Allen is the only blood relative you have left in this world. I'm not asking for miracles. All I'm asking is that you stop tormenting yourself with something you can do nothing about."

He grunted. "God, how I wish it would have been anyone else but her!"

She sighed. "Well, it is, and it won't change. I've been doing a lot of thinking, and I'm going to drop the charges against Maggie. Even if she weren't your sister, I would still be dropping the charges. I never did feel right about bringing them against her in the first place. She didn't react any differently than anyone else would have in her situation."

"I don't believe I'm hearing this! You're my wife, for God's sake, and your duty is to stand by me!"

"Brant, just think about this for a moment. How do you think a judge would see me if this goes to court? My credibility would be ripped to shreds."

"I don't think so. Maggie would be the one torn apart and deservedly so." He relaxed his jaw as his voice softened. "You're my wife, whom I happen to love very much, and your life was threatened. The judge will see it from that point of view and you'll win hands down. In this day and age verbal threats are not taken lightly."

"Win what, Brant? This isn't a contest. I want this to stop now. I can't take it anymore, and I'm going to have the charges against Maggie Allen dropped whether you like it or not! That's final!"

"No, Janna, you're not going to do anything of the sort. I'm your husband, and you'll do as I say! Case closed!"

Her eyes flashed. "Don't you dare speak to me in that tone of voice ever again. And don't you dare tell me what I can and can't do! I will drop the charges!"

"What did you say?" he insisted. "You would go against what I know is best?"

She determinedly tossed her head back and met his eyes, her blue one's angrily boring into his smoldering gray ones. "Yes, you heard me correctly."

"You're going to let that bitch come between us?"

Janna's lips slightly quivered. "Maggie's not the one coming between us. It's you, Brant. Can't you see that? I can't live like this anymore. I'm sorry your father made you feel like less of a person and constantly threw Maggie in your face. But now you know why he did it. You have to let go. I'm sick and tired of it. It's over." A tear slid from her eye. "I don't understand this anger of yours, and it frightens me." She grabbed a tissue and dabbed at her teary eyes. "I love you so much, but you've finally succeeded in pushing me right out of your life."

"Oh, no, honey!" He grabbed her around her slender waist enclosing her in his strong arms. "No, don't say that," he hoarsely whispered. His fingertips gently brushed the hot tears from her cheeks. "I love you so much! I couldn't live without you, Janna. Please don't ever leave me! I never knew what love was until I met you. Please don't ever leave me... promise me," he said in a cracked voice.

She didn't answer as tears continued to spill from her eyes. She clung to his strong back as he gently guided her to the bed. He tenderly laid her upon it, then softly and lovingly kissed and caressed her body.

CHAPTER TWENTY-TWO

Chris leaned against the doorjamb staring down at Chelsea. "I'm here, so what do you want to say?" he impatiently asked.

She looked into his eyes then quickly looked away. She couldn't bear the obvious hatred evident there, but worse, she knew the hatred was directed at her. "I need you to listen to this first." She took a shaky breath. "This is going to make you angry, but you need to hear it."

Chris raised his eyebrows. "I'm not in the mood for games, Chelsea. Maybe it was a mistake for me to come over." He turned on his heel.

"No, please, Chris. Just listen." She led him to the sofa. Before he could protest further, she pressed a button on her cell phone. "Just listen, please."

He sat down on the edge of the sofa. His face paled as he listened. He couldn't believe what his ears were hearing. When it had played through, he stared dumbfounded at her. "You...you deceiving, lying bitch! You've destroyed my life!"

He shook with rage.

Chelsea shuddered as she bit her lip. "I know I can't undo what I've done, Chris. I am sorry," she weakly replied.

"You're sorry?" He sucked in his breath. He felt like he'd just been kicked in the gut. "Brant Evans is the father of your child," he slowly spat out, "but you tried to get me to take responsibility. Why?" His nostrils flared. "What kind of woman are you, Chelsea? How could you do such a despicable thing? Answer me!" he raged. "How could you destroy me and Maggie?"

She choked on her tears. "I know what I did is the lowest thing anyone can do, and I know that I can never give you back the life you lost with Maggie." She sobbed. "Believe me, Chris, if I could change any of this, I would in a minute."

"Was Brant Evans worth it, Chelsea? Was he worth what you've done to Janna? How could you do that to your best friend?" He stood up, shifted his weight, and slowly walked toward her. "Do you even have a conscience? You've sunk as low as you can. You can't go any lower. Does that make you proud? What was the prize, Chelsea?"

She cowered in fear as he abruptly stopped in front of her then glared down at her. "I thought Brant cared about me," she sniffed. "I was such a fool. And, yes, Chris, I do feel guilty for what I've done to Janna." She trembled. "But if it's any consolation to you, Brant has used me and left me to deal with this on my own."

He scoffed. "Please don't ask me to feel sorry for you."

"I'm not, Chris. All I'm asking for is your help."

"My help?" he sneered. "Your child is not mine. I never intend to see you again."

"Just hear me out. Please, Chris." She swiped at her eyes as she drew a deep breath. "I'm going to come clean with

Janna and with Maggie. Maggie deserves to know what really happened, and when she listens to this then she'll also know the truth."

"I doubt she'll ever have anything to do with either of us, because it still doesn't excuse the fact that I did sleep with you that one night."

Her face reddened. "No, Chris, you didn't. We never had sex."

His mouth flew open. "But I remember having a few beers and then kissing you—"

She drew a long, shuddering breath. "Brant gave me something to put in your beer. After you were passed out, he came over, undressed you, and placed you in my bed."

Chris's heart jumped into his throat. "I never cheated on Maggie. I knew I could never cheat on her."

"She never deserved this, but maybe in some small way it will give her comfort knowing that you really were faithful to her."

Chris squinted.

"Especially now since she found out that Brant is her brother."

"What!" The blood rushed to his head. His head felt like it was ready to explode.

"Chris, you don't even know half of what's been going on lately." She motioned to the chair. "Please just sit down and listen."

He silently sank into the chair across from her. His head was whirling. "What's going on? How can Brant Evans be Maggie's brother? It doesn't make any sense."

Chelsea seated herself on the sofa and placed her trembling hands in her lap. "Believe me, I still find it incredible. If Janna hadn't told me, I never would have known."

****

Maggie drew a hot bath, lit some candles, and then popped a CD into the portable CD player. She gingerly stuck a toe in the water, and finding it to be of a comfortable temperature, stepped into the bathtub. She eased her body down into the luxuriating bubbles enjoying the light scent of jasmine, then rested her head against the back of the tub.

She sighed as she took a fingertip and slowly ran it through the bubbles. Soon she'd begin looking for a new home, but she didn't want anything fancy or high maintenance this time around. She'd become accustomed to the simple things in life and was determined to never go back to her previous lifestyle. Something small and cozy would suit her just fine. Maybe she'd even buy a small piece of land outside the city limits and build a small log cabin home. She pictured a creek in the back and all kinds of wildflowers. She'd even plant a small vegetable garden and have her own flowers growing everywhere. She smiled at the irony of how her lifestyle had completely reversed itself.

She closed her eyes reflecting on how bizarre life was. Never in a million years would she ever have imagined her mother to be capable of keeping such an enormous secret. At the same time, a deep sadness permeated her soul with the knowledge that she'd never known her biological father and never would. How fair was that? She'd never be privy to any personal information about him, only the information Nick Saunders shared with her. She'd never hear the stories of his boyhood from his own lips. She'd never know if she had inherited any of his traits. She focused on the soothing music, praying it would comfort her tormented soul, but she knew it wouldn't, not tonight anyway. She was wound tight as a clock, but it wasn't strictly because of her parents.

No matter how much she tried to convince herself otherwise, Chris Jacoby still had a tight grip on her heart, and she feared he always would. How strange life was. The man she truly loved could never be hers.

CHAPTER TWENTY-THREE

Jason Lightman nodded at Shelly and Maggie as he made his way over to where the two women stood.

"Is something wrong, Jason?" Maggie asked as her breath caught in her throat. She fearfully grabbed Shelly's arm.

A smile broke over his face. "No, I have wonderful news for you. Janna Evans has dropped her charges against you."

Maggie's eyes brightened as relief rushed through her. "She did? What happened to change her mind?"

"I received a phone call from her attorney early this morning informing me that she was withdrawing the charges against you. I'll know more once I receive the papers."

"What a load off your mind, Maggie," Shelly said grasping Maggie's hands.

"It certainly is, even though I didn't do anything to Janna in the first place. That still disturbs me."

"Maybe that's what changed her mind," Shelly reasoned. "Her conscience must have kicked in. At least we now know that she has one."

Jason laughed.

Maggie looked at Jason. "Oh, I'm sorry, Jason, I haven't introduced you two. This is my coworker and best friend Shelly Burgess."

Jason flashed a broad smile at Shelly. "I'm pleased to meet you, Shelly," he said extending his hand.

Shelly softly shook his hand. "It's nice to meet you too." She observed the rapidly filling diner. "I'd better get back to the customers before the natives grow restless." She smiled at Jason. "Thank you for bringing Mag some good news."

"I'll be there in a minute, Shell." Maggie said then turned her attention back to Jason. She saw his eyes following Shelly's departing form.

"She seems like a nice young woman," he observed.

"That she is," Maggie agreed. "She's a super woman, and she's doing a fantastic job of raising her two young sons by herself." She watched as his eyes flickered at the mention of Shelly's single status.

He nodded and then glanced at his wristwatch. "Well, I have to get to the office. I just wanted to stop by and give you the news in person. Give Tom my regards."

"Will do. Thanks, Jason."

****

Maggie softly hummed a popular tune as she made her way back to the grill.

Tom looked up from the pile of potatoes he was dicing for home fries. "I heard about your news. What a relief."

Maggie frowned. "Thanks."

"Why the long face? I thought you'd be ecstatic."

"I am happy it's over, but it still disturbs me that I was

203

falsely accused in the first place."

He placed the potatoes on the grill slowly spreading them out. "Maggie, I know you didn't do anything…everyone knows that. Put it behind yourself. Just move on, honey. It won't do you any good to dwell on it."

"I know, Tom, but I think I need to for just a little while," she answered with a wry smile.

He chuckled. "Well, I am happy it's over."

"I really am too. I just wonder what made Janna change her mind." She sighed. "By the way, Jason sends his best."

"He's a good man."

"Yes, he is." She was thoughtful for a moment. "Tom, can you tell me anything about Jason's private life? Is he seeing anyone? I assume he's not married since I never saw a photo on his desk or a ring on his finger."

Tom cocked a brow. "Are you telling me that you're interested in him?"

She laughed at the gleam in his eye. "Not in that way. But I think he may be interested in Shelly."

A broad smile broke over Tom's face. "Did he say something to you to give you that impression?"

"It's what he didn't say."

"Well, what do you know? I think they'd make a perfect couple."

"My thoughts exactly." Her eyes twinkled.

"What's up your sleeve?" he asked.

Maggie pursed her lips. "I'm formulating a plan. As soon as I figure it out, I'll clue you in."

He chuckled as he turned the potatoes. "I can only imagine."

****

Brant grabbed a beer then stomped into the living room. He

sat on the sofa and removed his boots, propping his feet upon the coffee table at the same time grabbing the TV remote. He flicked through a few channels then turned the TV off. There wasn't anything worthwhile on this early in the morning. He opened his beer and took a long swallow. He was tired, but his tiredness wasn't from physical labor. His mind was whirling. He didn't know if or when Chelsea might spill the beans to Janna. He was sitting on a powder keg and he had to prepare himself to have a reasonable, but more importantly, believable explanation for Janna. He looked up when Janna walked into the room. Her beauty was arresting. Any man would be a fool to cheat on her. But he realized a long time ago that he didn't fit the norm of being just any man. He made his own rules. So far, he'd gotten through life just fine too.

He was a much-hated man. He knew it but it didn't bother him. What bothered him was to be a much-hated man whom no one feared. He smiled at his wife, his eyes brightening as she seated herself next to him.

"Have a tough night, honey?" she softly asked. "You look exhausted."

He shook his head. "No, just the usual. It's mentally fatiguing enough without having to work the graveyard shift."

"Why did you take this shift?"

"I knew that Jack had some family things going on, so I decided to give him a break."

"That was a nice thing to do." Her eyes narrowed suspiciously. "But why did you switch? Since you have seniority, surely someone else would have switched shifts with him."

He smiled. "That's true, but I have another reason."

"And that would be?"

He grinned as he drew her closer to him. "This weekend I'm taking a couple of extra days, and you and I are going away by ourselves. We need and deserve the break."

"Oh, honey, thank you!" she squealed as she threw her arms around his neck.

"I love you so much, Janna. I never want anyone or anything to come between us."

"Nothing ever could," she murmured close to his ear.

He stiffened. "But there are those who will try."

"Who, Brant? Has something happened?"

He grunted. "It's Chelsea."

"Chelsea. Why would Chelsea want to come between us? She's my best friend."

He rubbed his tired eyes. "She called me at the station last night." He shook his head back and forth. "You wouldn't believe the ridiculous things she said."

Janna frowned. "That doesn't sound like Chelsea. I know she's been extremely upset lately, but why would she take it out on you? You two have always been so close."

"I know, but it just goes to show how greedy even your friends can be when they find out you've come into a little money."

"No, that doesn't make any sense at all. Chelsea's always known that I have money, and she's never acted jealous." She frowned again. "Tell me what she said, Brant."

"It's going to upset you, honey."

"I want to know everything she said, Brant. I'm your wife and if my best friend has a problem with you, then she has a problem with me."

He wearily exhaled. "She's blackmailing me. If I don't give her some money, then she's going to tell everyone that I've been having an affair with her and am the father of her child."

Janna patted Brant's shoulder. "That's ridiculous. Why would Chelsea make up such a horrible lie? What purpose is she hoping to serve?"

The muscles in his jaw twitched. "I don't know."

"I know she's been having problems with Chris. He's gotten cold feet and isn't willingly making his way to the altar. But to make such horrible accusations against you. How could she do this to me? Pregnant or not, I'm going to give her a piece of my mind."

He tenderly touched her cheek. "No, sweetie, just stay away from her."

"No, Brant, I've got to set things straight with her."

Brant's eyes narrowed. "She's manipulative. I should have seen it coming. She uses dirty tactics to get what she wants."

"But why, Brant? Why would she want to alienate me, especially now in her condition?"

He shot her an incredulous look. "Money is her motivation. It's as simple as that."

"It still doesn't make sense. You really think she would stoop to do something so low?"

"Women like her will do anything to get their hands on a fortune without caring who or what they have to use."

"What about Chris?"

"He walked out on her and his unborn child. She's mad at the world and has chosen me to take her revenge out on."

Janna's eyes sparked as she snuggled closer to Brant. "She won't get away with it," she promised.

****

Chris picked up his steaming thermos of coffee and poured out a cup, then screwed the top back on. He had a long hard day ahead of him, and he struggled with his mind to force his body to spring into action, but his body seemed to be winning the battle. Exhaustion seeped from every pore in his body.

"Feeling all right?" Bill Jenson asked, concern evident in his voice. "You don't look so good, boss." He carefully eyed him.

Chris took a gulp of his coffee. "Just a bad night, that's all. I'll be okay after I get my hit of caffeine," he replied with a weak laugh.

Bill studied him. "Anything you want to get off your chest?"

"No thanks, Bill. I'll work it out."

"Well, if you need to talk, I'm here."

"Thanks." Chris slapped him on the back. "What is your crew going to do first?"

"We've got to plow up the meadow. That's going to take the better part of the morning. I'm hoping to get the first section of concrete in before day's end, though."

"Sounds like we're right on schedule," Chris said pleased.

"If it doesn't rain for a couple of days…" Bill called over his shoulder as he walked back to his men.

"Nah, we've got a few days before any storms come in." He rubbed his burning eyes. He promised Chelsea he'd give her a call later this morning. Last night after he had some time to absorb everything, his first instinct had been to locate Brant and wring his scrawny neck.

After he calmed down some, though, he realized that the only logical thing to do was talk to Maggie, together with Chelsea. The problem was figuring out a way Maggie would allow them that opportunity. She couldn't be blamed for never wanting to see either of them, but once she learned that Brant was the force behind this, maybe she'd soften just a little. Especially since he never had cheated on her in the first place. At least he hoped she'd soften up.

He couldn't change the past, but he damned well knew that he could change the future. Brant Evans would never destroy another life. He'd swear on his last breath that if Brant ever hurt another soul, he'd kill him himself with his own bare hands.

CHAPTER TWENTY-FOUR

Chelsea paced the floor, impatiently waiting for Chris's phone call. She was exhausted, hardly able to get a wink of sleep last night. Every time she drifted off, a horrible nightmare quickly awakened her. A nap this morning she thought would help, but after trying fruitlessly for half an hour, sleep still eluded her.

Her stomach gave a violent lurch, and a smile broke across her face as she moved her hand to her stomach. Guilt washed over her as she realized how this innocent child she carried in her womb had been used to harm and deceive so many others. She had to set things right. Her child deserved to come into this world without the encumbrances of these deceptions. How she wished things could have been different and this beloved child was coming into this world with two parents who loved him instead of only one. Yes, she did love him, and yes, she desperately wanted him and ached to hold his tiny body in her arms. She would give her child enough love to make up for the lack he would never receive from his father.

Brant Evans should never be allowed to father any child, but she intended to hold her head high and let anyone who cared to know that Brant was the father of this baby. If he chose to ignore his own flesh and blood, then that would be a decision of his own making, but her child would know the truth.

****

Chris reluctantly punched in Chelsea's phone number then put his cell phone to his ear. "Hi, Chelsea, it's me."

"What have you decided to do, Chris? Do you want to get together later and see Maggie?"

"No," he slowly said. "Give me a couple of days. I need to think about it some more. Remember, this is still new to me too."

"I know," she guiltily replied. "Just let me know."

"I will," he promised. "One more thing, Chelsea…guard that phone with your life."

"Of course."

Chris was right. He deserved to take as much time as he needed. She was grateful that he was even civil to her after what she'd done. But now was the time for her to come clean on her own. She grabbed her car keys and hurried out of the apartment.

****

An hour later Janna ushered Chelsea into her living room. She pasted a phony smile on her lips. "It's been so long since we've had a nice long chat."

After she was comfortably seated on the sofa, Chelsea nervously looked at her. "It hasn't been that long."

211

Janna couldn't help but notice Chelsea's lost, sad expression. As angry as she was with her, though, her sympathetic side toward her friend overpowered her. "Is everything all right with the baby, Chelsea? You look like you've just seen a ghost." She grabbed Chelsea's clammy hands. "What's wrong? Can I get you something?"

Chelsea shook her pretty head. "No, Janna. I…I need to tell you something." Her voice wobbled. She bit down so hard on her bottom lip that it bled. "Please hear me out."

Janna's brow puckered. "Why so serious? You're acting like you're about to deliver devastating news." She prepared herself for the worst. Maybe Chelsea was here to apologize for what she'd said to Brant and ask Janna's forgiveness. Yes, that had to be it, Janna reasoned.

Chelsea lowered her eyes. "How has Brant been acting lately?"

"Brant? He's been wonderful. In fact, we're going away this weekend. He's a changed man. I think he's finally got his priorities straight. It's been a rocky road, but we're both determined to work at our marriage. We never want to lose one another." She rested her hands in her lap. "Is there something you want to tell me?" she softly asked.

Chelsea swallowed hard. She raised her eyes and met Janna's questioning gaze. "The road is still rocky, and you're just about to hit a boulder."

"What are you talking about? You're not making any sense at all. Does this have something to do with Chris?"

"Yes, Janna, and it has everything to do with Maggie and Brant."

"What's going on, Chelsea? What's happened?"

Chelsea slowly put her hands in front of her eyes. "Oh, God, Janna, I'm so sorry," she moaned.

Janna sighed. "I already know. Why did you say those horrible things?"

"What? You know? How?"

"Brant told me." She leaned forward. "Chelsea, I don't know what's going on with you and Chris, but if you needed money, why didn't you just ask me? You know I'd do anything to help you. I thought we were friends. You don't know how hurt I am."

"I don't know what you're talking about," she answered.

"Brant said you called him at the station and tried to blackmail him. I understand you're having a rough time in your personal life, Chelsea, but why would you stoop to such a low level?"

"I never tried to blackmail him. He's lying, Janna. You have to believe me."

Janna's friendly attitude quickly changed. "Just because you are miserable, why do you feel the need to destroy my happiness? Friends don't do that to one another. Quite frankly, Chelsea, I'm offended and disappointed with you."

Chelsea's eyes widened. "Brant's been lying to you all along."

"I don't want to hear anything further. I don't trust anything you say. I think you'd better leave now, Chelsea." She got to her feet.

Chelsea grabbed her arm. "Janna, please, just listen to me. I have proof."

"Proof?" she scoffed. "What proof?"

Chelsea removed her cell phone from her pocket. She sucked in her breath. "Before I play this for you I want you to know that I've already played it for Chris."

"Just play it," Janna demanded.

Chelsea hit the play button.

****

Shelly sat at the counter sipping a cup of coffee as she flipped through the pages of a magazine.

Maggie slid onto the stool next to her. "All set for tonight?"

"Yes, Tom's coming over at seven."

"Good." Maggie excitedly clasped her hands together. "We have to be here at seven-thirty."

"This is a beautiful thing you're doing for Tom."

"Well, Shell, you know that if it wasn't for him giving me a job, I don't know what I would have done. He's a wonderful man." She looked into Shelly's bright eyes. "And even with everything that's happened I wouldn't change any of it, because meeting you and Tom turned out to be the best thing that's ever happened to me."

Shelly swallowed hard. "You're so sweet, Maggie." She blinked back tears.

Tom sauntered over to them. "Oh no, what's going on?" He looked at Shelly's tear-filled eyes.

She laughed. "Nothing's wrong, Tom. We're just both so happy."

He scratched his head. "Women."

"Yeah, but you love us," Maggie teased.

"Yeah, yeah, yeah," he snorted good-naturedly. "If you girls are about ready, I'll lock up."

"Okay," Maggie said and slid off the stool. "See you tomorrow, Tom."

"Good night, Maggie." He turned to Shelly. "I'll see you in about an hour."

"Thanks again for doing this, Tom."

"It'll be a treat for me."

****

214

Janna shivered uncontrollably. "I…I," she stuttered.

Tears streamed down Chelsea's cheeks. "I couldn't go on with this lie. It was eating me alive." She sniffed.

"Why? Why?" she screamed. "What did I do to you to deserve this?" Her face crumpled as tears splashed down her pale cheeks. "What kind of monster are you?"

"I'm so sorry. I know nothing I do or say matters, but if I could take it all back, I would."

She looked at Chelsea's bulging stomach. "You're carrying my husband's child," she moaned. "Get out!"

"I don't want to leave you this way." Chelsea moved toward her.

"Stay away from me! Get out!" she screamed.

****

Maggie showed the contractors out of the diner, then locked the door. The work would be done in about six weeks. That would give her plenty of time to formulate her plan to bring Shelly and Jason Lightman together. She would enlist Tom's help and that way she'd be accomplishing two projects at once. Tom would never suspect that she had another motive for getting him out of the diner while the work was being completed. She smugly smiled, proud with herself.

"Well, I guess I'd better get home so Tom can get to bed. We don't need an old grouch on our hands in the morning," Shelly joked as they walked to their cars.

Maggie laughed. "I can't wait to see the look on his face when the work's completed," she said as she opened her car door.

"It's going to be hard controlling my excitement the next several weeks."

"I know," Maggie agreed. "But the wait will be well worth

215

it."

"What's on your agenda for the rest of the night?"

She took a deep breath. "I'm going to see Nick Saunders."

Concern creased Shelly's brow. "Is everything all right?"

"As much as can be. I still have so many questions about Roger Evans." She paused. "My father…it still sounds strange to say it aloud."

CHAPTER TWENTY-FIVE

Brant's eyes smoldered as he gripped a mug of coffee.

David Dennings sat across from him. "I guess we can file this report in the closed case file," he said with a sound of relief in his voice as he pushed the folder toward Brant. "What do you think?"

Brant opened the folder and quickly scanned the contents without comprehending the words on the report. His mind was elsewhere. "Yeah," he said setting his mug down. He pushed the folder back to Dennings.

Dennings picked up the folder and took his time opening the filing cabinet before placing the folder inside. "So why the sour mood?" he asked with his back to Brant.

"Chelsea's threatened to talk to Janna," he snarled.

Dennings eyebrows shot up. "I wouldn't worry too much. Janna would never believe her. She's nuts about you."

"Chelsea is her best friend. You know how women tend to stick together." He frowned. "Besides, what if Chelsea tells

217

her about the baby?"

Dennings turned around with a wide grin on his face. "Come on, Brant, you can easily have that taken care of."

He thoughtfully rubbed his jaw. "You're right." He laughed loudly. "You're right!"

****

Maggie's brow furrowed. "I need to find out more about my father. There are so many unanswered questions."

Nick Saunders set a steaming cup of coffee in front of her.

"This might sound like an odd question, but do I look anything like my father?"

He smiled. "You're as beautiful as he was handsome. Besides his looks, I believe you've also inherited his calm nature and sensitivity to others."

She ran a hand through her hair. "If you had known me when I was in the corporate world, I think you would have had a much different opinion of me."

Nick leaned back in his chair with his eyes firmly fixed on her. "Maggie, I know all about your past. I also know that your kind, trusting nature was what put you in that unfortunate situation."

She blushed. "Thank you, Nick." She sipped at her coffee then set the cup back down, staring thoughtfully into it for a few seconds. "I didn't know how much finding out that Roger Evans was my father would impact my life. I don't know how I could have thought that news wouldn't change anything inside of me, but it has." She looked up. "Now I feel the need to know everything about him." She laughed self-consciously. "I wonder if he had any of the same quirks I have. I know everything I inherited from my mother, and I used to think it strange that I seemed to inherit nothing from the man who I'd always known as my father."

Nick quietly listened as she talked. "Your feelings and questions are understandable, and I'll do my very best to answer all of your questions. I may even be able to answer some you haven't even thought about." He smiled brightly.

Maggie cocked an eye. "Lately I feel as though I'm stuck in the middle of a heavy fog."

"I don't know if I'd be as calm as you now are if I were in your place."

"I may look calm on the outside, but believe me, I'm an emotional wreck on the inside."

"Would you like to see some pictures of Roger?" he asked. "He left a photo album in the event you might want to see it."

Her eyes grew bright. "I'd love to. Thank you."

****

Brant opened the door and quietly slipped inside. He flicked on the light then walked into the kitchen and grabbed a beer from the refrigerator. He pulled out a chair and sat down, at the same time pulling the tab off his can of beer. He took a long swallow. Beads of perspiration popped out on his forehead.

He sat in the silence, consumed in his own thoughts and turned startled when he heard footsteps. They stopped at the entrance to the kitchen.

Janna stood stony-faced but silent. He prepared for the worst.

"Hi, honey. I tried to be quiet so I wouldn't wake you." He quickly stood up, almost knocking his chair over. His jaw twitched nervously.

Her rigid stance didn't change.

"Tomorrow night we'll be at the inn," he said with a smile. "I'm looking forward to it. Are you excited, honey?"

219

"No, Brant," she stiffly replied. "I'm filing for a divorce."

He grabbed her arm. "A divorce?" he hoarsely said. "What's wrong, honey?" His heart thumped loudly in his chest. "Where's this coming from?"

"Why don't you ask Chelsea?"

"Was Chelsea here? I warned you about that lying, conniving bitch!"

"Who's the liar?"

"You're accusing me of lying?" he incredulously asked. "I can't believe I'm hearing you say that. You're going to believe her over me, especially after I warned you about her?" He felt the sweat drip into his eyebrow.

"You can't lie your way out of it."

Her calm tone scared him. "What did she say?"

"It's not what she said. It's what I heard."

Brant watched as her face slowly twisted and contorted and her true emotions began to erupt. Her eyes revealed the pain she felt. He held his arms out to her. "You're not making any sense. She had no right to come here and upset you."

"Get away from me," she moaned. "Don't you ever touch me again!"

"Honey, please tell me what she said to you."

"I heard the conversation you had with her. She taped it, you son of a bitch! You're a lying, scheming bastard!"

Brant ran a shaking hand over his jaw as he feebly sought an answer. "I made a mistake. It was a one-time thing and I promise it'll never happen again. We can work this out, Janna. We're a team, remember? Just give me a chance. Everyone deserves a second chance." He was sweating profusely. "We'll get counseling."

"Get out!" she hissed. "The sight of you makes me want to vomit!"

He grabbed her shoulders. "We can move away. We'll make a fresh start," he begged. "Just say you forgive me. It'll never happen again."

"I said get out...now!"

****

Chelsea stirred, listening in the still, heavy darkness. She frowned as she turned on her side trying to find a comfortable position. The sound she'd heard which had awakened her must have been a remnant of a dream. She strained her ears, but all was quiet. She had just closed her eyes again when she heard the noise. She raised herself to a sitting position, pulling the sheet to her chin.

It was unmistakable this time. The familiar tapping at her door, the tapping she used to jump with joy over now frightened her. She ignored Brant's knocking, hoping he would soon go away. But he didn't go away. He persisted with the taps, which soon turned into loud pounding.

She silently slipped out of bed and ran to her closet, huddling deep within the shadows. Her heart leapt into her throat when the shattering of glass and a heavy thud sounded from the living room. He'd smashed through the window. She trembled in fear.

The heavy footsteps were making their way through the apartment. She listened as her possessions were smashed and sent crashing to the floor. The desk drawers were yanked out and she listened to the ruffling of papers being strewn about. As the footsteps drew closer, she huddled further back into the closet. She desperately tried to squelch her panic-stricken, heavy breathing. Perspiration dripped down her back as the footsteps continued to come closer. She placed a hand on her stomach as they stopped outside the closet door. Why hadn't she thought to grab her cell phone off the nightside table?

A wrenching, knife-sharp pain tore through her abdomen. She covered her mouth with her other hand, desperately trying to contain the screams that rushed to her lips. She couldn't let him know she was here. She prayed he would leave.

She squeezed her eyes shut, but the throbbing refused to subside and seemed to worsen. She shrieked as her stomach heaved violently. In a few seconds the throbbing pain had subsided, but something was wrong. She feared for her baby's life at this moment more than she did for her own.

Brant swiftly yanked open the closet door. His flashlight cast a soft beam of light as he trained the light toward the back of the closet. A strong hand parted the neatly hanging clothes. He grabbed the string attached to the light switch, quickly pulling it and instantly flooding the small room in light.

Chelsea squinted as her eyes became accustomed to the brightness. She shrank further back into the tight space with her back solidly against the wall. Brant's shadowy, massive form stood in front of her. Her eyes traveled down to his black, steel-toed boots. Her eyes moved up his body, resting on his face.

He stood quietly staring at her. The twisted smile on his lips and the wild, haunted look in his eyes convinced her that Janna had confronted him.

"Why are you hiding?" he calmly asked. "You're not afraid of me now, are you?"

Her voice froze in her throat.

"Do you know that you've destroyed me?"

"No, Brant, I didn't," she croaked, unnerved by the contrast between his sinister expression and his relaxed voice. "All I wanted was for you to want and love our baby as much as I do." She gritted her teeth as another shooting pain, but with less intensity than the first, shot through her. "I need to get to the hospital. Will you drive me?" she panted. "Something's wrong."

His lips turned into an ugly smile. "I don't care about that bastard," he snarled, eyeing her stomach. "I don't care if it lives or dies!"

"No, Brant, you don't mean what you're saying." She shook as she tried to reason with him. "We conceived him out of love...our love."

"I know exactly what I'm saying." He grabbed her shoulders, roughly pulling her to her feet. "You couldn't follow a simple plan."

The sudden movement, combined with his hot breath smelling of stale beer, gagged her.

"Don't you dare puke on me!" he bellowed.

She tilted her face toward the floor just as the vomit gurgled up her throat and spewed out of her mouth.

Brant moved back a step but not before his boots were splattered. He lunged forward, pushing her away.

Chelsea was propelled backward, and she struggled to maintain her balance. She landed with a dull thud against the back of the closet. A bloodcurdling scream tore from her throat, echoing in her ears as though it had come from someone else. She got on her knees. She had to get to a hospital. Sweat ran from every pore dripping into her eyes. "Help me, Brant," she moaned.

"Shut up, you dumb bitch!"

"It hurts so bad, Brant, please help me," she panted.

A sharp kick to her stomach sent her sprawling. With both hands, she grabbed her midsection.

Chapter Twenty-Six

Chris dialed Chelsea's number. When her cell phone went to voice mail, he hung up without leaving a message. He rammed his hands into his pockets as he surveyed the work site. He breathed a heavy sigh of relief. This job was right on target, and soon his personal life would be too.

"How's it going, Boss?" Bill Jenson asked sauntering toward him.

"Right on schedule. Let's hope this good weather holds."

Bill removed his hard hat. "Is everything else okay?"

Chris grinned. "Yeah."

He cocked an eyebrow. "Have you talked to Maggie?"

Chris's forehead creased. "Not yet, but I intend to very soon."

Bill thoughtfully studied him for a few seconds. "Are you going to tell me about your sudden change of mood or are we going to play a guessing game?" he jokingly asked.

"I've got wonderful news!" He slapped his friend on the

back. "I'm not the father of Chelsea's baby. You'll never guess who is."

"Congratulations!" Bill squatted as he tossed his hat onto the ground and then picked up his thermos of coffee. "Okay, this has got to be good. I'm officially on my break now. Would you like some?" He motioned toward the thermos.

"No, thanks." He sat on a tree stump. "The one and only Brant Evans is the father."

Bill pulled on his chin. "Well, well, so the plot thickens."

"You've got that right. He conned Chelsea into his sick, devious plot. She's no innocent by any means, but at least I now know the truth, and soon Maggie will too."

"What's his motive?"

"To get what he wants. Chelsea and I are going to talk to Maggie, hopefully tonight."

"I hate to put a damper on your good mood, but what makes you think that Maggie will believe anything Chelsea tells her?"

"Chelsea figured out that Brant was only using her. The last time he came to see her she got incriminating evidence on tape. He can't get out of this one."

"Wow! Chelsea's smarter than I would have ever given her credit for."

Chris laughed. "Yes, she is. We're going to convince Maggie to listen to it. But there's even more."

"I'm all ears."

"Chelsea admitted to me that I never touched her. In reality, I never did cheat on Maggie in the first place. She drugged me."

Bill took a gulp of coffee. "This is like one of those soap operas my wife watches."

Chris chuckled. "Who would ever believe it?"

"It'll be a happy day when you and Maggie are finally together again."

"I'm going to do everything humanly possible to get her back, and when I do I'll never allow anyone or anything to ever come between us again."

****

Brant groaned as he pulled himself to his feet. He stretched his stiff limbs and walked to the grimy window, peering at the dismal sky. The dark, gray sky matched his mood. He pulled a razor from his desk drawer.

He had almost finished shaving when David Dennings sauntered over to him. "What the hell happened to you? You look like shit."

Brant cocked a bloodshot eye at him. "Well, buddy, let me put it to you like this. I've been to hell, and now I'm trying to come back."

"What are you talking about?"

"Janna threw me out last night. Chelsea got to her."

"Come on, Brant, you can sweet talk Janna. Just lay some of that charm you're famous for on her. In a couple of days I'll bet she comes begging you to come home."

He shook his head. "No, I'm afraid nothing I do or say will change things. It's over. She'll never forgive me for fathering Chelsea's baby." He ran a hand threw his hair.

"Pull yourself together, man. You're not thinking straight." He carefully eyed him. "Is there more than you're telling me?"

"No, I'm just tired. I slept in the backseat of my car last night." He shrugged. "I had a few hours to kill so I thought I'd come in and catch up on some paperwork."

"You need sleep."

"What I need to do first is find a place to live. I'm going

226

to call Janna and make arrangements to pick up some of my things." He pulled on his jaw. "After my head clears some, I'll figure out what the next step is."

****

Janna finished pulling Brant's clothes from the closets and dresser drawers. She wiped the sweat from her brow with the back of her hand, not caring whether it was ladylike or not. She'd worked at a feverish pitch, her adrenaline keeping her hands busy. She picked up a framed photo of him and gazed at it for a few seconds before hurling it into a wall. Her chest heaved and she slumped to the floor. "Damn you, Brant! Damn you, Chelsea!" she screamed.

She swiped at her blurry eyes then pulled herself to her feet. No, she refused to cry over either of them. They weren't worth her tears. They were two of a kind and deserved one another. The phone rang, startling her in the silence of the large room. She answered it before it could ring a second time.

"Janna, it's Brant. We need to talk."

She swept her hair from her puckered brow. "There's nothing to talk about." Her voice was cold. "In fact, I've spent most of the morning getting your things together."

"Let's not end it this way," he softly implored. "We need to give us another try."

She shrilly laughed. "You've got to be joking! I had all night to think about the pros and cons of life with you. What you did is unforgivable. I could never trust you again, Brant. You have no scruples. How would you expect me to react if we ran into Chelsea and her child somewhere, knowing that you're the father? Or didn't that ever enter your self-centered mind?"

"Just give me one chance, and I promise I'll make it all up

to you. We can try to have a baby of our own. We'll put this mess behind us," he pleaded.

"No, Brant. I don't give second chances. It's over. You can pick up your things. I'll be out all afternoon." When she heard no response from him, she wondered if he'd hung up on her. "Brant, did you hear what I said?"

"Yes," he answered in a calm voice. "I heard every word you said."

"I'll be seeing my attorney tomorrow to begin divorce proceedings against you."

"That's your final word?"

"It is."

"Well, in that case, don't forget to remind him that I never signed the prenuptial agreement. Remember, it was at your insistence."

Janna slammed the phone down. She trembled with anger. He wouldn't win. She refused to let him win. Not this time.

CHAPTER TWENTY-SEVEN

Chris tried Chelsea's number off and on throughout the day. An uneasy feeling gnawed at him. At quitting time, he jumped into his truck and drove over to her apartment.

He knocked on the door. He felt something crunching under his work boots and looked down at some broken glass. His eyes shifted to the picture window, the draperies moving in the gentle breeze. One end was caught on a piece of jagged glass. He cupped his hands over his eyes and peered inside.

"Chelsea!" he shouted as his pulse quickened. He raced back to his truck, grabbed his cell phone, and called 911.

He nervously paced back and forth in front of his truck, every few seconds stopping to peer down the street. Every minute seemed like an hour. The world felt like it was going in slow motion as panic gripped his soul. He was overcome with an intense feeling of dread.

He breathed a heavy sigh of relief when a patrol car sped to the curb and two officers jumped out. He was glad that

Brant wasn't one of them. He couldn't deal with his sarcasm tonight. But if the truth were known, he didn't know if he would be able to physically control himself if he set eyes on Brant at this moment. He hurriedly filled the officers in, then followed them to the porch.

Dennings glanced at his partner then cautiously moved toward the broken window. "It's a mess in there."

Officer Dirk Samuels tried the door. "Well, we've got an open invitation," he said pushing the door open.

Chris walked behind them as they made their way inside the apartment, his fear mounting as they slowly walked from one ransacked room to the next. He was visibly shaking when they reached the bedroom. His eyes scanned the familiar room and suddenly stopped, riveted on Chelsea's twisted body, which was lying halfway in the closet.

"Chelsea!" he called rushing to her side. "My God!" he frantically called. "Look at all the blood! Call an ambulance… hurry!"

"Don't touch anything," Dennings ordered. "Please wait outside, Mr. Jacoby."

Samuels radioed for an ambulance as Dennings secured the area. "I said wait outside!" Dennings barked.

Chris's eyes flitted nervously back and forth as he looked from Chelsea then to Dennings. "I need to explain a few things to you."

Dennings abruptly stared him in the eye. "What do you know about the break-in?"

"I don't know anything about the break-in, but I know someone who had it in for Chelsea."

"What are you doing here?" he suspiciously asked.

"I came to talk over some personal business with Chelsea."

"What kind of business?"

Chris rubbed his jaw. "She was mixed up in an affair with a married police officer."

"From Cedar Pines?"

He nodded.

"And just who is this officer?"

Chris hesitated a moment before answering. "Brant Evans."

Dennings scoffed. "I think you've got your facts wrong." He put his face so close to Chris's that Chris thought in a moment they'd be rubbing noses. "You'd better watch what nasty rumors you start floating around or you might find yourself in a serious slander trial!" His eyes narrowed. "Now wait outside!"

Chris turned just as the paramedics rushed into the room. He hovered in the doorway as the men rushed to Chelsea's side. He impatiently shifted his weight from one foot to the other as he leaned his frame against the door.

The paramedics stood up and looked at Dennings. "She's dead. She may have been dead for hours."

Chris walked on what felt like stilted legs to where she lay. "No, she can't be!" His voice was hoarse.

"Jacoby, I told you to get out of here! But don't go far," Dennings warned. "I'm not finished questioning you."

Chris numbly made his way to the small entrance porch. He placed his hands on the rail and sucked clean, fresh air into his lungs. Chelsea was dead, and there was nothing he could do to bring her back to life. He shivered in the cool night air. He'd never forget the image of her battered, bloodied body. As much as he'd despised her, she and her baby didn't deserve to die this way. No one did. A tear slid from his eye. She was just a kid, for God's sake, with her whole life in front of her.

231

His hands tightened on the porch railing. The smell of death lingered in his nostrils. He'd never smelled death before. He wished he never had.

****

Dennings threw the report on his desk then plopped into his chair. He fixed his eyes on Brant's bent head.

Brant scribbled something on a report then looked up, his face brightening. "What? You should be happy that I've made a dent in the pile." He motioned to the stack of files on his desk.

Dennings looked skeptically at him. "What's going on, Brant?"

He frowned. "I might be able to tell you if I knew what the hell you're talking about."

"You haven't heard about Chelsea?"

"I haven't heard anything about anyone. After I picked some of my stuff up from my house, I saw a realtor. There's a cabin out on Highway 97 for rent. I drove over and looked. It's a beauty...nice and secluded." He grinned from ear to ear. "I can't move in for a week or so. In the meantime, I rented a room and crashed for a few hours. I got here and everybody was rushing around because of the drug bust at Barber's Tavern. So I sat myself down and thought I'd be doing my partner a favor by getting some of this damned paperwork caught up."

He pulled on his chin. "It's bad news, Brant."

"What's the little tramp done now? Made more threats?"

He shook his head. "It was the worst sight I've ever seen. She's dead, Brant...murdered."

"What!" His eyes widened. "Chelsea murdered? I don't believe it. Any suspects?"

Dennings leaned back in his chair. "I questioned Chris

Jacoby. He was the one who reported the break-in."

"There you go!" He pounded a fist on the desk. "He should be the prime suspect. After all, he had motive," he said pointing a finger at Dennings.

"I've questioned him. I don't think he had anything to do with it."

Brant shook his head. "You're wrong. I'll stake my life on it. Jacoby is your man."

"Come on, Brant, this is me you're talking to," he whispered. "If anyone had motive, it's you and you know it. Level with me. I'm already covering your ass."

"There's nothing to tell. You either believe me or you don't." He took a deep breath. "Just make sure I don't become a suspect."

"I'm not a magician. I've already got the boss convinced that it's a random act of violence though. Someone who knew she lived alone and would be an easy target."

"Just keep going on that presumption, and we'll all be happy."

"Jacoby may be a problem. He's shooting off his mouth about you and Chelsea and how you set her up."

Brant chuckled. "I'm sure you warned him of the consequences if anyone gets hold of his lies."

"He's been warned."

"Good." He studied Dennings. "I don't have to worry about you saying the wrong thing now, do I?"

His jaw twitched. "I never have."

****

Chris wiped his mouth then splashed cold water on his face. His throat burned. He didn't think he'd ever stop throwing up. He needed to talk to someone. He needed Maggie. The eleven o'clock news would be filled with coverage about the murder. Would everyone think he was guilty? He'd been trapped into a relationship with her, and most people assumed he had fathered the child she was carrying, the child inside of her that had died along with her. A tear slid from his eye.

Suddenly an overwhelming sadness enveloped him as he thought of that innocent soul whom Chelsea had so looked forward to bringing into the world. It was odd, but he now realized why the child had grown to mean so much to Chelsea. She had someone who would love her unconditionally. They'd died together. His lips trembled as more tears slid from his eyes.

****

Maggie settled into her favorite chair with a bowl of popcorn in her lap. She turned on the TV just in time to catch an old movie, one of her favorites. She sat for forty-five minutes enjoying her program when a news bulletin flashed across the screen. "Damn," she muttered aloud. "Just when it's getting to the good part."

She stayed in her chair hoping the news flash would be a short one. She halfheartedly listened as the newscaster announced a murder investigation was underway. Her heart leaped into her throat when Chelsea stared back at her from the television screen. "Oh my God!" she said as the bowl of popcorn slipped from her hands. She was shocked by the gruesome details.

With a shaky hand, she picked up her cell phone and punched in Shelly's number. "Hi, Shell, it's Maggie," she breathlessly said without giving Shelly a chance to respond. "Did you hear about Chelsea?"

"No, Maggie, what's happened?" she worriedly asked.

"She's been murdered. It was just on TV."

"Murdered! My God! Do they know who did it?"

"The police think it is just a random act, maybe someone looking for money for drugs. They are urging the public not to panic."

"That's horrible."

"I know. As much as I didn't like her, I still would never wish that on anyone." She paused. "Chris must be going through hell."

"Maggie, why don't you call him?" she sympathetically suggested.

"I want to, but I just can't." She shivered. "I wonder who did it."

"Mag, you don't think the police will suspect Chris, do you?"

Shelly had asked the question Maggie was afraid to ask. "What would you think if you were the police?"

****

Janna slipped into bed praying she would drift into a peaceful slumber. She needed to escape from the sadness and betrayal, if just for a few hours. Sleep was the only way she could accomplish that. After fluffing her pillow for what seemed like the hundredth time, she turned on the TV. She channel-surfed, then settled on the late-night newscast.

She set the sleep timer and then settled back onto her pillows as she slowly closed her sleep-deprived eyes.

"Chelsea Howard was bludgeoned to death. The police have no leads," the reporter's deep voice boomed, seeming to echo in the otherwise quiet room.

Janna bolted upright staring in disbelief at the screen. "It can't be," she mumbled. "No!" she screamed, piercing the darkness, when she saw Chelsea in happier times smiling back at her from the large screen.

Chapter Twenty-Eight

Maggie and Shelly quietly waited on their customers, neither woman feeling in the mood for small talk this morning. The customers' usual morning chitchat, joking around and bantering, wasn't there this beautiful, sunny morning. All their minds could think about was the senseless murder that had taken place. Maybe they wouldn't have been so emotionally affected if they'd heard that she'd been involved in a car accident, but to have been murdered in cold blood and her and her unborn child left to bleed to death was something no one could comprehend.

During a lull, Tom called Maggie to his office. He closed the door. "I know what you're thinking," he softly said.

"I don't want to think it, Tom, let alone believe it, but what about the police? Don't you think Chris will be their prime suspect?"

"Honey, we all know that Chris is incapable of harming anyone." His face brightened. "Besides, if the police suspected him, then why hasn't he been arrested?"

"Maybe they're waiting to get back some evidence. He was pushed so much, maybe he reached his breaking point. Everyone is capable of crossing over that line if they're shoved too hard."

"No," Tom disagreed. "Not Chris Jacoby."

****

Bill wiped the sweat from his brow and then refastened his bandanna. "I know you had nothing to do with it, Chris. So does everybody here." He slapped him on the back. "Besides, you heard the tape. I'll stake my life on it that Brant had something to do with it."

"I can't get the sight of Chelsea just lying there so still, out of my mind." A faint smile passed his lips. "I was hoping she'd get up and start bitching at me or something." He looked into Bill's sympathetic eyes. "There's no doubt that Brant did it. He had everything to lose."

"Do you have a copy of the recording?"

"No. I should have gotten a copy, but I was so mad when I heard it that it was the last thing I thought about."

"Well, maybe the police will find her cell phone. That will give them the proof against Brant," he optimistically said.

"I'm not counting on it. If they find the phone, I'm certain it'll come up missing or be destroyed before anyone gets wind of it."

"But you know, Chris. You can come forward and tell them about what Chelsea recorded on her phone."

"Why would they believe me? They'd think I was making it up to save my ass."

"Did Chelsea play it for anyone else?"

"I don't know."

Bill was thoughtful for a minute. "What about Brant's wife? Wasn't she going to play it for her?"

"I don't know if she ever got the chance. If she did, do you think Brant got confronted by Janna and in a rage went to Chelsea's apartment?"

"There you go. That's the only logical explanation. Why don't you contact Janna and feel out the situation?"

"Will you hold down the fort?"

"You've got it, boss."

****

Chris rang the bell as his eyes surveyed the immense, perfectly manicured front lawn and the beautiful landscaping of Janna's home. It was an enormous house with prominent columns at the entrance, and the long, winding driveway was lined with beautiful trees. It was like something out of a storybook, he thought.

Janna pulled the massive door open. "Chris," she said with a look of surprise on her face.

He looked into her red, swollen eyes. "Can I talk to you for a few minutes, Janna?"

She nodded as she held open the door then led him down a large, magnificently decorated entrance hall, then paused before the sitting room.

He sat in a stiff, upright chair. He nervously cleared his throat. "I don't really know how to ask you this under the circumstances."

She gave him a pointed look. "I'll regret until the day I die my final words to Chelsea," she sniffed. "If your question is about the cell phone recording, Chris, then yes, I heard it."

He looked around the room.

"Brant isn't here, in case you're wondering. I threw him out that night."

"I'm sorry," he replied. "I mean, I'm sorry for what Brant has done to you."

"Chris, you don't need to apologize to me. You and I have had our worlds turned upside down because of him, and now Chelsea is dead."

"She didn't deserve it."

"No, no one deserves to die like that. To think that someone brutally took her life is unforgivable." She swallowed the lump in her throat. "Have you talked to Maggie about the recording?"

"No, Chelsea and I were making arrangements to see her. I...I was there when her body was found," he choked.

"Oh, Chris, that must have been horrifying." Her lips trembled.

He took a deep breath and cleared his throat. "It was. I don't think I'll ever get that image out of my mind." His eyes blurred. "Janna, since you've heard the recording, would you be willing to talk to Maggie with me? I'll understand if you don't want to."

She sniffed. "Of course I will, Chris, but I doubt she'll listen to me. Remember, I had charges preferred against her."

"She'll listen. We have to make her listen. Her life was also screwed up because of the deceit."

Janna briefly closed her eyes then opened them again. "Chris. I'm doing it, not only because it's the right thing to do, but because I think that's what Chelsea would have wanted." She clasped her hands tightly together. "I said some horrible things to her."

"We all did," Chris said gently.

CHAPTER TWENTY-NINE

Brant finished moving the boxes into his new home. "So what do you think?" he asked.

Dennings wiped his hands on his jeans. "What a view! You were lucky to find this place."

"Yeah. I'm putting in an offer to the owners. I love it. No one near for a mile on either side. It doesn't get any better than this."

Dennings sat on the porch rail. "I destroyed the cell phone."

"Good."

"How the hell did you get the big boys to shift their focus away from Chris?"

He shrugged. "I just pointed out that it didn't make any sense. If he'd done it, then why in hell would he come back? It didn't help that he passed the lie detector test either." He chuckled.

"So now the focus is on some punk looking for drug

money."

"Yeah." He lit a cigarette and thoughtfully blew the smoke out. "I'll have to invite you and the guys out for a party as soon as I get settled."

"I thought you gave those up a couple of years ago when you went on that health kick."

"I did too, but I guess some habits are hard to break. It helps with the stress and there's no one to nag me about how bad they are to my health."

Dennings glanced at his watch. "The wife will bitch if I don't make it home in time for dinner tonight. The in-laws are coming over." He rolled his eyes.

"That's something I never had to worry about."

"Lucky you." He stood up. "Have you heard anything from Maggie?"

"Nah. I'll have to think up a reason to pay her a visit one of these days though. I've been keeping a low profile for the time being." He smirked. "I still think the money she got isn't rightfully hers. Now I'll just have to come up with a way to take it from her."

"Be careful." He nodded. "Well, I'd better be off."

Brant stretched his aching muscles. "You know what I'll be doing."

"That's what I'm afraid of…scheming. Watch your step, Brant. I might not be able to cover your ass the next time."

****

Maggie sat thumbing through the realtor brochure she'd picked up on her way home from work. She circled a few homes that might be a possibility to purchase. None of them, though, had quite what she was looking for, but she'd know the moment she saw the home that was meant to be hers. Her thoughts drifted to her parents. Lately, that's all she could think about. Finally, she was able, with Nick Saunders help in filling in the gaps about her father, to find some peace and even understanding. The anger had left her, and now she could move on with her life.

She jumped when she heard a knock at her door. She hurried to it peering out through the screen door. Her eyebrows lifted in surprise at the sight of Chris and Janna.

"Maggie, can we please come in?" Chris asked in a low voice. "We have something we need to talk to you about."

She unlocked the door and motioned them inside, narrowing her eyes in question at Chris as Janna passed her.

Chris nervously rubbed his jaw. "I was planning again to ask to speak to you, but then you know, everything with Chelsea happened."

Maggie nodded. "Please accept my sympathies."

"We didn't come here for that," Janna broke in. "First, I want to thank you for allowing me into your home after what I've put you through. You're a much more gracious woman than I would ever be under the circumstances."

"Please have a seat." Maggie gestured to the sofa.

Janna settled herself on the sofa, and Chris plopped down on the arm of the sofa as Maggie sat in her easy chair.

"I know this isn't a social call," Maggie said trying to make her voice light. "So what do you two want to talk to me about?"

Chris shot a glance in Janna's direction.

Janna took a deep breath then slowly let it out. "It's no secret that Brant is capable of committing the most unspeakable acts toward others." She twisted the strap of her handbag. "I've left him, Maggie."

"If this is the place that I'm supposed to say I'm sorry, I

just don't have it in me."

Janna smiled weakly. "No, it was the smartest decision I've made. I left him because he fathered Chelsea's baby, not Chris."

"What!"

"Chris never touched Chelsea. It was a setup that Brant masterminded and coerced Chelsea into after she'd become pregnant by him. I never understood Brant's dislike of you, Maggie, until the truth came out about your blood ties."

"I thought Brant didn't know anything about that until he was given his inheritance."

"He didn't. but his father had thrown your accomplishments up to him ever since he can remember. So he took his nastiness out on you. But when he found out you were his half-sister, he was like a crazy man ranting and raving. He wouldn't let it rest. It pushed him over the edge."

"I appreciate you telling me this, Janna. I'm sure it hasn't been easy on you." Her voice was kinder now.

"He used Chelsea, too, only she outsmarted him when he dumped her. She secretly recorded him on her cell phone. He couldn't lie his way out anymore. She played it for Chris and me. Chris and Chelsea were making plans to meet with you to play it for you when she was murdered."

Maggie sat frozen in her chair. She didn't know what to say or think. "Where's the cell phone now?" she finally asked.

Chris frowned. "We don't know. The only conclusion we can come up with is that the police probably found it."

"If that's the case, then it will never come to light." Maggie directed her attention to Janna. "No offense."

She shook her head. "I'm a fool to have ever believed the stories Brant told me."

"That's water under the bridge now," Maggie quietly said.

"You had a right to know, Maggie," Chris said. "I know you need time to let this sink in, but I swear to God I never slept with Chelsea."

"She told me the same thing she told Chris," Janna confirmed. "Chris was drugged, and Brant undressed him and placed him in Chelsea's bed."

"That's not the issue now. The issue is who do you two think killed Chelsea?" She knew by the looks in their eyes that they suspected Brant the same as she did. "He needs to be stopped!"

CHAPTER THIRTY

Maggie was perspiring profusely as she hoisted another large bag of flour onto the storage shelf. "At least I'm building some muscles," she joked.

"I don't like you doing this heavy work," Tom scolded. "Let me hire someone to do the heavy lifting."

"It's not that heavy," she said with a wink. "Besides, this physical labor gives me a chance to let off steam."

"Why don't you take a break now, Maggie?" he said leaning against the door to the storage room.

She rubbed her hands on the back seat of her jeans. "I want to get this inventory finished tonight."

He walked around the room. "It looks great in here. I don't think I've ever seen it so organized."

She grinned. "Yeah, Shell and I busted our tails all day."

He rammed his hands into his pockets. "You're working too hard lately. Why don't you go out and spend some of that money on something you'd really like for yourself."

"I already have." She grinned.

He cocked an eye at her. "Oh yeah? What'd you buy?"

She tucked her shirt into her jeans. "I'm getting a new car next week…nothing fancy. I'm also going house hunting."

"Good for you! It'll be nice to see you in a decent home." His face reddened. "Not that you didn't keep the trailer nice."

She laughed. "I know what you mean, Tom. But I'm thankful that at least I had a home." She looked sideways at him. "But I do believe any day now it's going to completely fall apart, especially when those winter winds come howling through"

He chuckled. "I'm glad you've managed to maintain your sense of humor through the past few weeks."

"If I hadn't, I don't think I would have survived." She frowned. "I just wish Chelsea's murderer would be brought to justice. But it looks like it will be a cold case file."

"He'll trip up someday. His kind always do."

"Not Brant Evans."

"Even Brant Evans," Tom disagreed. "Someday one of his cronies will turn on him, and all hell is going to break loose. Mark my words."

"It would be nice." She lifted another sack.

"Did Shelly have a date tonight?"

"She refuses to call it a date. Some guy from her church asked her and the boys out for pizza. She says he's nice enough, but she just doesn't feel anything more than friendship for him."

"Jason is definitely interested in her, but he's hesitant to ask her out."

"Why?"

He shrugged. "He hasn't had much luck with women, but I've noticed he's been stopping in more frequently for coffee."

"Well, I took the liberty of asking him to dinner at Shelly's tomorrow...without her knowledge of course."

"Nothing like being subtle."

She smiled. "Someone had to do it."

Tom scratched his chin. "Have you spoken to Chris at all?"

"Not since the night he and Janna came to the trailer." She pushed a loose strand of hair from her brow. "He's called a couple of times, but I'm just not ready. I'm sure the day will come when I'll talk to him, but I honestly don't know if I'll ever want to get back with him."

Tom smiled as he stared at her. "You're not a very good liar, Maggie."

****

Tom settled himself on Shelly's sofa. "Thank you for inviting me to dinner."

"You're family, Tom. You know that. Besides, how many times have I invited you and you always had an excuse for not coming?" she chided.

He grinned. "You're right, but I've changed. Life's too short." He glanced around the large room. "I love this house. Every time I come over you've done something new."

"Thanks. I really enjoy fixing it up. Next year I'm thinking about putting a deck on."

"That'll be nice," he answered as the boys came bursting into the room.

"You're here! Yippee!" Terry exclaimed.

Tom spread his arms out. "Come here, you two."

"Hey, Shell, I'm here," Maggie called as she opened the door. "I've brought a guest."

Shelly blushed as she looked at Jason.

"I hope it's not an inconvenience," Jason said, hesitating by the door.

"No, not at all." She relaxed and smiled broadly. "I'm happy you could come."

Maggie caught her eye and winked, causing Shelly to turn even redder than she was.

Tom stood up rushing over to Jason. "It's good to see you, Jason. Let me introduce you to these two handsome young men right here. This is Tommy," he said placing a gentle hand on top of Tommy's head. "And this is Terry."

Jason squatted down to their level. "It's nice to meet you two."

The boys shyly smiled.

"So I hear that you two like going to the zoo."

"Yeah!" they squealed.

"That's our most favorite place in the whole world," Tommy said stretching his arms out. "You can come with us next time," he invited.

"Yeah, can he, Mommy?" Terry asked looking at his mother.

Shelly blushed again. "If he wants to, he can."

Jason grinned at Shelly. "I think I would like that."

****

Later Maggie stood at the sink washing dishes as Shelly dried them. "That was a fantastic dinner, Shelly."

"Thanks." She set a plate on the counter. "You're something else, Maggie Allen. Do you know that?"

She shrugged as she scrubbed a pan. "Hey, someone had to get you two together."

"He's asked me out this next weekend."

"Oh, Shelly, I'm so happy for you."

"I hope you can find happiness again someday, Mag," she

sincerely said.

She sighed. "I am happy, Shell. For the first time in my life, I feel content. I've done a lot of soul searching the past few months and I've gotten to really know myself, and I like the person I am. I guess that's the secret. When you have a clear conscience, everything else just seems to fall into place. It's a peace I haven't known in my entire life."

"I still don't know how Brant Evans can live with himself." Her lips drew tight. "I heard he's got a different woman every weekend at his place. Janna must be so humiliated."

"I think he's looking to get a hefty sum of money from the divorce."

"He strikes again," Shelly said through gritted teeth. "Like he needs any more money. He makes me sick. I can't stand the way he swaggers into the diner expecting everyone to bow down to him. And I certainly don't like the way he looks at me like he thinks if he wants me he can have me whether I agree or not," she angrily said. "The last time he came in, he groped me. But of course it's his word against mine."

"Calm down, honey, the creep's not worth working yourself up over."

"I can't stand what he did to you and Chris. I'd like to wring his neck."

"I survived and as far as I know, Chris is surviving too. Brant will get his."

"The sooner the better," she fumed.

****

Later that night they stood in the middle of Tom's Diner. "I can't believe this! I'm speechless!" Tom stuttered.

"It's not finished, but this is the start," Maggie excitedly said as she and Shelly threw their arms around his neck.

249

"It's beautiful," he said in a cracked voice, "but you shouldn't have." He cleared his throat. "I'm just overwhelmed."

"You don't have to say anything, Tom. It's about time you received some reward for all you've done for me and Shelly," Maggie said.

He held up his glass. "To my family. May we always be together," he said.

Epilogue

Brant struggled to cry for help through the blood gurgling in his throat. But even if he could have screamed, no one would have heard him.

Janna had already gone, leaving him to slowly die alone.

Try out another story by Susan K. Droney
Now Available
The Stalker

Susan K. Droney
AUTHOR

Writing is Susan's number one passion. When she isn't writing, she enjoys reading, spending time in her garden, and visiting family and friends. She has many novels, short stories, and magazine articles to her credit. Raised in western New York, she now resides in New Jersey. For information about Susan's current and upcoming titles, please visit http://www.susandroney.com or http://susandroney.blogspot.com